MW01257512

BAKER STREET BY-WAYS

Other titles available from
Otto Penzler's Sherlock Holmes Library

Sidney Paget's drawing of Holmes and Watson for
The Boscombe Valley Mystery in *The Strand Magazine* of
October, 1891 — the first appearance of the 'deer-
stalker'

BAKER STREET BY-WAYS

James Edward Holroyd

OTTO PENZLER BOOKS
New York

Otto Penzler Books
129 West 56th Street
New York, NY 10019
(Editorial Offices only)

Simon & Schuster Inc.
Rockefeller Center
1230 Avenue of the Americas
New York, NY 10020

Manufactured in the United States of America

10   9   8   7   6   5   4   3   2   1

Library of Congress Cataloging-in-Publication Data

Holroyd, James Edward.
    Baker Street by-ways/James Edward Holroyd.
        p.   cm.
    1. Doyle, Arthur Conan, Sir, 1859–1930—Characters—Sherlock Holmes.   2. Detective and mystery stories, English—History and criticism.   3. Holmes, Sherlock (Fictitious character)   4. Private investigators in literature.   I. Title.
PR4624.H58 1994   94–9285   CIP
823'.8—dc20

ISBN 1-883402-71-9

ACKNOWLEDGEMENTS

Thanks are due to the editors of the *Manchester Guardian, New Statesman*, the *Cornhill* and the *Sherlock Holmes Journal* for permission to reprint some part of the material which appeared in their publications.

ILLUSTRATIONS

1. Sidney Paget's drawing of Holmes and
   Watson for *The Boscombe Valley Mystery* frontispiece

2. Regent Street   facing page 48

3. Wyndham Robinson's evocation of Sidney
   Paget drawings   49

4. Northumberland Avenue   64

5. Bow Street   65

6. 'The ever-changing kaleidoscope of life . . .'   80

7. Pall Mall   81

CONTENTS

1.	Profile	9
2.	One Man's Pilgrimage	15
3.	How It All Began	28
4.	Sidney Paget's Drawings	38
5.	Dorr Steele and Some Others	44
6.	Where Was 221B?	53
7.	Solutions by Numbers	68
8.	Fanciful Furnishings	75
9.	'Our Sanctum'	81
10.	The Shaggiest Dog	87
11.	Sherlock Holmes in Regent Street	92
12.	Pistol Packing Partners	98
13.	Dr Watson and Mr Wilde	103
14.	A Baker Street Portrait Gallery	114
	Dr John H. Watson	115
	Mrs Hudson	123
	Mycroft Holmes	126
	The Yard	130
	Colonel Moran	136
	Horace Harker	138
	Irene Adler	141
	Henry Baker	142
	Dr Lysander Starr *et al*	147
	The 'Exploits'	153

BAKER STREET BY-WAYS

Profile

The Sherlock Holmes story I should like to write would open conventionally — but where else? — in the famous sitting-room at 221B Baker Street. Dr Watson would, as usual, be peering out of the bow-window. Holmes, also as usual, would be engaged in one of those noisome and completely incomprehensible chemical experiments. Watson would then remark that they were about to have a visitor as a tall man was approaching the door. Holmes, naturally without looking up from his work, would mutter: 'Six-feet-two. Seventeen-and-a-half collar. Plays cricket.'

The door-bell would ring. Holmes, again in character, would remark that here, if he mistook not, was their client's foot upon the stair. The door would then be flung open dramatically. Framed in it we should see — not the oscillating reptilian head of Professor Moriarty, not the huge Dr Grimesby Roylott, 'his face burned yellow with the sun and marked by every evil passion' — but a tall, broad-shouldered good-humoured figure reminding one of Big Bob Ferguson or the Missing Three-quarter.

Holmes, on cue as always, would say: 'Pray be seated. I perceive from your large boots that you are a policeman; from the traces of cotton fluff upon your sleeve that you are from Manchester; and from your visiting card that your name is — er — Acco Nandollay.'

9

To which the visitor would briskly retort: 'Holmes, I am afraid you are losing your grip. I am a doctor, not a policeman; what you imagine to be fluff is really the pattern of the suiting; I live in London, not in Lancashire; and my name is not Acco Nandollay but A. CONAN DOYLE.'

Brought together at last, the three men would go on to discuss the shape of future stories. Not very original, I fear; for the trick of allowing the characters to step out of the page is as old as *Treasure Island*. Nevertheless the encounter would have an edge of reality — particularly during this year of the Conan Doyle centenary — since all three would doubtless be somewhat baffled by the world-stature of the legend they have achieved.

One can imagine a measure of asperity in Holmes' comments on that page of Conan Doyle's notebook of the mid-eighties in which the author casually named his detective 'Sherrinford' Holmes and set down Watson not less improbably as 'Ormond Sacker'.

Holmes and Sacker, forsooth!

But these infelicities never got into print. Although the author was blandly unaware that he was filling in the birth certificates of a pair of immortals, he appears to have been conscious of the inadequacy of first thoughts. So Holmes eventually took his front name from a cricketer against whose bowling Conan Doyle had once knocked up a good score; while the slightly Firbankian Sacker gave place to a real Doctor Watson who had been one of the author's early friends at Portsmouth.

Thus invested, Holmes and Watson met at Bart's Hospital in 1881, took over the famous rooms at 221B Baker Street, and started on the series of adventures which was to hold generations in thrall and set the pattern for in-numerable followers.

The first story, *A Study in Scarlet*, appeared in Beeton's Christmas Annual in 1887. Conan Doyle sold it outright for £25; yet a single copy of this rare shilling book-let will today change hands for as much as £150. The second, and much better, Holmes novel, *The Sign of Four*, was commissioned for Lippincott's Magazine at a small dinner party to which Oscar Wilde was also invited. At this meeting Wilde also undertook to write *Dorian Gray*. Conan Doyle's story appeared in 1890 with the title *The Sign of* the *Four* — a form which American editions still use.

It was in the newly-established *Strand Magazine* in 1891, however, that Sherlock Holmes began to grow in stature and to give full play to those amazing, and occasionally fallible, powers of deduction which were to keep poor Watson's head awhirl with bewildered admiration. In that incomparable series of short stories the figure of the great detective (modelled in part on Conan Doyle's former pro-fessor at Edinburgh University and in part on his own remarkable capacities) was filled out until it became more real than many of his flesh-and-blood contemporaries. Violin and pocket lens were already familiar from the two earlier novels, but dressing gown and pipes, hunting crop and ear-flapped cap — these and a score of similar touches showed him in the round. So, too, the setting. Those solidly uncomfortable armchairs, that massive and so-evident dining table, the bearskin rug, the corner for the chemical apparatus — all these became, and for large numbers of people have remained, as immediately recog-nizable as the furniture in the homes of close friends. And it is against this background that enthusiasts tell over the titles of an evocative litany: *A Scandal in Bohemia, The Red-headed League, The Speckled Band, The Blue Carbuncle, Silver Blaze....*

But although the triumphs of Sherlock Holmes were beginning to bestride two continents, his creator was less than happy. Holmes, notwithstanding his genius, got in the way of the larger historical canvases which Conan Doyle, and indeed some of his readers, always felt to be his appointed work. 'He takes my mind from better things,' the author wrote to his mother. So, on May 4, 1891, Holmes ('the best and the wisest man whom I have ever known,' as Watson mournfully recorded) was committed to the abyss of the Reichenbach Fall in Switzerland, locked in the arms of his arch-enemy Moriarty. And there Conan Doyle intended to leave him; for when Stephen Gwynn mentioned Holmes to the author about that time, the reply was 'Thank God I've killed the brute; don't let me hear a word about him.' To countless homes in the England of the far-off nineties this must have seemed the ultimate betrayal.

Yet never was detective more indestructible. After a pause of eight years the publication of *The Hound of the Baskervilles* sounded a welcome note of reminiscence; and when the first of the *Return* stories appeared in the following year (1903) and it was seen that Holmes was really alive the day, with queues outside the *Strand* offices, must have been jubilant indeed. Conan Doyle had been knighted in 1902 and it was felt — perhaps not entirely frivolously — to be due as much to the reappearance of Holmes in the *Hound* as to the author's public service in rallying world opinion on our conduct of the South African war.

Thereafter the great detective's career was treated with

the distinction it so well deserved. Every new adventure was given pride of place in the old *Strand Magazine* to which Holmes remained undeviatingly loyal. On the stage he had already been brilliantly portrayed by William Gillette, the American actor, and in later years he was to dominate the screen at the hands of Arthur Wontner, Eille Norwood, Basil Rathbone and others. Not without honour in his old parish of Marylebone, a mews was named after him just around the corner from his familiar headquarters in Baker Street. This gesture was a kind of compensation, for there was already a Watson's Mews elsewhere in the borough. Small wonder that a party of Continental schoolboys said they wished to begin their tour of London with a visit to Mr Holmes' house or that a French general asked Conan Doyle during the First World War whether Sherlock was serving in the British army.

Holmes was above all the man of his period and that period was indubitably the nineties. His setting is the London of jingling hansoms and rattling fourwheelers (why did Holmes and Watson never take a bus?), of ulsters, fogs and gas-lit streets; and in so far as some of the later stories and drawings occasionally step outside this framework with telephones, typewriters and once, incredibly, a motor car, they have been regarded as so much the less appealing. An old Cornish fisherman was indeed fumbling for the clue when he told the author that while Holmes may not have been killed in the precipice incident he was never quite the same man afterwards. But this contention would be resisted by many of the experts; not least by the late Sir Arthur Conan Doyle himself.

Holmes retired to bee-keeping in Sussex in 1903; his last emergence was to outwit the German spy Von Bork in

August 1914; and the final story (*Shoscombe Old Place*) appeared in the *Strand* as long ago as April 1927. Yet in these succeeding years his fame has steadily grown. Books have been written, clubs established, magazines founded, radio, film and television appearances regularly staged, exhibitions organized, even a ballet presented — all in honour of Holmes and Watson. But with a difference. The modern fashion is to engage in a little detection oneself. Thus it is possible to begin reading, or re-reading, merely for pleasure and to be drawn into amiable argument. The enthusiast who casually embarks on, say, *The Adventure of the Priory School* may soon find himself an active member of the *a priori* school. Escapism either way, of course; but at least in the good company of the reader's hero; for Holmes once confessed that his life was spent in one long effort to escape from the commonplaces of existence.

It is a measure of Holmes' universality that the 60 stories which make up the saga should continue to be the object of such undiminishing affection and tireless research and that the balance should be so well held, in the phrase of an American woman writer, 'between solemn nonsense and tender legend.' It is perhaps even more because of his power to call forth these qualities than for the conquest of crime in the London of his day, that many of Sherlock Holmes' followers would subscribe to Watson's description of him as 'a benefactor of the race'.

One Man's Pilgrimage

One fine Sunday morning years ago I walked with a friend in Marylebone. I had been reading Vincent Starrett's *Private Life of Sherlock Holmes*. As we turned out of Baker Street into Paddington Street I suddenly saw a passage on the opposite side of the road labelled 'Sherlock Mews'. I almost whooped aloud, for I at once pictured Conan Doyle strolling in the same quarter in the mid-eighties. He ruminates on his new characters. The Baker Street domicile is exactly right, but he is a trifle unhappy about 'Sherrinford' Holmes. Sherrinford Holmes? Shirley Holmes? And then Conan Doyle turns into Paddington Street in the direction of his later consulting rooms in Devonshire Place. His eye catches the magic name 'Sherlock Mews' and — a star is born.

All this was in my mind as I hurried across Paddington Street for a nearer confirmation on that distant Sabbath day. But alas for literary detection. A fading sign, stencilled on the wall, read 'Sherlock Mews: late York Mews South'. The mews had been named after the detective and not, as I had rashly hoped, the detective after the mews. This experience marked the beginning of many excursions into the by-ways of Baker Street. The journey is as endless as it is enthralling and in this year of Sir Arthur Conan Doyle's centenary, in fellowship with Sherlockians the

15

world over, I acknowledge its source with gratitude and affection.

'There will be some study which every man more zealously prosecutes, some darling subject on which he is principally pleased to converse; and he that can most inform or best understand him, will certainly be welcomed with particular regard.' Thus Dr Johnson. I take it as text in the hope that one man's account of his pilgrimage to Baker Street may lead others to the same road and the same rewards.

Like most aficionados, I first encountered Holmes in boyhood; by good fortune in bound *Strands* in the home of one of my friends. My first adventure, *The Hound of the Baskervilles*, at age eight or nine, coincided with my first ghost stories. The double spell has never been broken; it can be evoked with all its overtones of terror merely by repeating the occult title of the book. But strangely I did not re-read either Holmes or Conan Doyle in general, although during youth one of my closest friends used to quote bits from the Conan Doyle short stories and two others actually wrote to the author — but about fairy photographs, not ghost hounds.

For some years my only Sherlockian volumes were a pocket edition of the *Memoirs* and one early volume of the *Strand*. The rest I had read from borrowed or library copies. Around 1930 I became aware that the sacred writings, as the Americans called them, were being critically examined; but even after I had acquired Vincent Starrett's book and seen the light, so to speak, in Sherlock Mews, I still retained my complacency, composure, call it what you will: was still somehow partially deaf to the subtle siren-song of 221B.

One Man's Pilgrimage

I date my complete capitulation from the publicity given in December 1949 to the impending demise of the *Strand Magazine*. The evocative reproduction of some of the early Christmas Number covers sent me back to a total re-reading of the stories. In this pietic exercise I was nobly friended by my wife who immediately presented me with the two Murray omnibus volumes and any others we could find — a gesture she is apt to regret when the place becomes ankle-deep in Sherlockiana. The next month — January 1950 — I remember a fine article by Chris Morley in *The Sunday Times* in which he said exciting things about the Baker Street Irregulars of New York and how he would rather have their quarterly journal than 'a first Bristol Cream of Wordsworth and Coleridge's "Lyrical Ballads" '. Then and there I resolved to acquire a set.

During the year I wrote a piece about Sidney Paget and his drawings. By this time I had begun collecting like mad. I ruined a short stay in Buxton by failing to snap up the first twelve volumes of the *Strand* — in pristine condition — for 17s 6d the lot. Soon after returning to London, however, I was well compensated in acquiring the volumes 1–28 in half-leather for £2 5s od. Her ladyship thought less of the transaction than I, for it involved making a two-bus journey across London on a wet Saturday afternoon and humping two coolie-like consignments to the nearest request stop.

While brooding over the Paget article I called in Marylebone Reference Library one day to consult some Sherlockian books of reference. The material was patchy when one remembered that Holmes lived in the parish for so many years. As I recall, there were no first or illustrated or unusual editions; no run of the *Strand Magazine* con-

taining the stories with the original drawings. But, in-
valuable for me, they had the three precious volumes of
The Baker Street Journal as well as Bell and Blakeney. I spent
an entranced afternoon among these treasures. It was perhaps then that I realized that the vision of this romantic
Holmesian world could be seen as clearly, shared as en-
thusiastically, in the U.S.A. and other countries as around
the corner in the Master's own Baker Street.

My call at the library, though sufficiently casual in its
origin, was not without consequence. For during conversation with Jack Thorne of the reference staff, I suggested
that Marylebone should put on a Sherlock Holmes exhibition for the Festival of Britain celebrations in the following
year (1951). I believed that whereas people would not
cross the street to see the usual municipal display — however laudable — of slums cleared and schools built, they
might even cross the Atlantic in pursuit of their hero. The
idea was duly discussed by the Marylebone Library Committee and was debated by the Council on October 26,
1950. There was some opposition and muttering about
'this fictitious figure associated with murky crime'. In fact
this resistance movement was enormously valuable, for it
brought an immediate wave of newspaper publicity in
support of the great detective. Pre-eminent was the series
of sixteen letters, and a leader, in *The Times*, in which
Mycroft, Lestrade, Mrs Hudson and other notable
characters came out of retirement to follow the lead of
John H. Watson, M.D., late of the Indian Army, in hoping
that 'second and better thoughts would prevail'. Prevail
they did and it cannot be doubted that Dr Watson's letter,
written by my old friend Ian Leslie, editor of *The Builder*,
provided a timely and perhaps a crucial rallying point.

During following months my exhibition idea flowered into something rich and strange. Councillor Robert Sharp, subsequently Mayor of Marylebone, inspired the reconstruction of the 221B sitting-room which, under the careful hand of artist Michael Weight, gave a focus to the whole show. Professor W. T. Williams, now of Southampton University, produced a learned section of specimens throwing new light on such matters as the identity of the speckled band and the lion's mane; Anthony Howlett lined a wall with photographs from stage and screen; Lord Donegall discovered the solitary cycle; Winifred Paget contributed some of her father's original drawings. Sherlockian societies overseas showered the exhibition with literature and greetings. It was duly opened in the Abbey Building Society's headquarter, Baker Street on May 21, 1951, by Dennis and Jean Conan Coyle, who, with their brother Adrian, had loaned many priceless items. The exhibition ran triumphantly until the autumn; was seen by Queen Mary and 54,000 other visitors; was then transferred to New York with Jack Thorne as its irrepressible curator; and has now found permanent anchorage in the re-named Sherlock Holmes tavern near Charing Cross.

The London Sherlock Holmes Society founded by the Rev. Dick Shepperd and A. C. McDonell in 1934 did not survive the War. It was therefore natural that a few enthusiasts should meet one summer evening during Festival Year to launch a new body — the Sherlock Holmes Society of London. We were housed in a committee room in Marylebone Town Hall and I recall that the pads of buff scrap paper which had also been provided bore on the reverse side the legend: 'Marylebone Road Convenience. Men's Department.' It could have been read as a comment on the movement.

The Society was vastly fortunate in securing S. C. Roberts, then Vice-Chancellor of Cambridge University as president; in enrolling Ivar Gunn (as chairman), Sir Gerald Kelly and Ivor Back, who had all been members of the earlier group; and in attracting such authorities as Dr Maurice Campbell (*Holmes and Watson: a Medical Digression*), Guy Warrack (*Sherlock Holmes and Music*), Gavin Brend (*My dear Holmes*) and Sir Paul Gore-booth (who holds a high Mycroftian post at the Foreign Office).

A well-known man-of-letters who attended the first meeting feared that the society might die of inanition. 'The canon is fixed: there can be no new discoveries,' he told me. Well, after eight years the society flourishes; has upwards of 150 members, meets half-a-dozen times a year, produces a journal and has links with similar bodies in many parts of the world. And what, it may reasonably be asked, are the functions of this eminently crack-brained group? I cannot give a better answer than to quote from the constitution of the society: 'to bring together persons who have a common interest as readers and students of the literature of Sherlock Holmes; to encourage the pursuit of knowledge of the public and private lifes of Sherlock Holmes and Dr Watson; to publish the transactions of the Society and communications dealing with the Sherlock Holmes canon.'

In this pursuit members light-heartedly combine the thoroughness of Holmes himself with the constancy of Watson and the tenacity of Lestrade. For example, before the late Gavin Brend gave a talk on the travels of the blue carbuncle, he undertook the journey himself — on foot. It carried him over five London boroughs and he was probably correct in his modest assumption that this was a world record since it was unlikely that any other person had ever covered precisely the same route. Norman Crump, city editor of *The Sunday Times*, also followed Mycroft's exhortation to go to the scene of the crime — advice which the great bureaucrat seldom followed himself! — and made a risky investigation of the Underground tracks around Gloucester Road and Aldgate in an attempt to find whether the Tube train bearing the body of Cadogan West on its roof was travelling clock-wise or the reverse. (*The Bruce-Partington Plans.*) On a sweltering summer evening of 1952 about fifty members gathered on the north side of Cavendish Square and allowed me to guide them along the mews and passages of the 'empty house' route. One of the highlights of that excursion — which properly ended in a meal and a discussion over maps in a first-floor room looking down into Baker Street — was that I was able to show the party a V.R. letter-box in Chiltern Street. This was obviously the place where Holmes would post his mail (it is significantly only a few yards from Nos. 109/111) and, as the late Jim Montgomery subsequently suggested, it probably inspired Holmes to trace those patriotic V.R.'s on the wall of the sitting room.

The society has been closely linked with the installation of various commemorative tributes to the Master. The first of these, outside the old Criterion Bar in Piccadilly Circus where Watson met the immortal go-between who was to introduce him to Holmes, unhappily disappeared soon after it was formally presented. Nor, despite the efforts of Lestrade and Gregson's successors, has it been restored. The plaque was subscribed for by American and British Sherlockians in the U.S.A. and Tokio, and while its removal was doubtless nothing more than a display of undergraduate high spirits, it seems regrettable that thousands of visitors should be deprived of seeing this testament to the greatest of all detectives at the very hub of the scene of his most notable triumphs. If the present possessor will see the incident in this light, I shall be very willing to meet him at the 'Sherlock Holmes', the 'Alpha Inn', the 'Bar of Gold', or some other appropriate rendezvous and receive back the precious plate — with no questions asked.

When the Society was firmly established I suggested to Norman Crump, one of our railway experts, and the late Ivar Gunn that it might be a suitable gesture for us to offer to present the nameplates so that a 'Sherlock Holmes' locomotive could again glide through the Master's local station. An approach was made to a senior executive of the London Passenger Transport Board. He, like the 'Retired Colourman', was naturally 'helpless in the hands of the two experienced man-handlers' and so the thing was accomplished. The nameplates of the original locomotive were removed during the drive for scrap-metal in the last War; but on October 5, 1953, the Society's president broke a bottle of Beaune across the bows of the re-named engine and a good muster of members climbed into the first coach and travelled to Finchley Road Station to inaugurate the first journey. The speed, of course, was $53\frac{1}{2}$ miles an hour. The Transport Board had provided specially-printed Baker Street Station tickets for the event; and at an earlier meeting a deerstalker had been passed round to help defray the cost of the plates. The member who remarked that the locomotive ought to have been steam, not electric, was referred to the adventure of *The Missing Three-quarter*: 'We progress, my dear Watson.'

A third commemorative plate, also presented by an

American society, was subsequently set up in Bart's Hospital as near as could be judged to the site of the laboratory where Holmes and Watson were first introduced and the first deathless words exchanged, 'You have been in Afghanistan, I perceive.' They are as familiar to the world as 'Dr Livingstone, I presume?' — and fifty times more exciting. There was surely something visionary in this scene from the first chapter of the first story as Holmes put hand on heart 'and bowed as if to some applauding crowd conjured up by his imagination'. But it is unlikely that there will be any more plaques. We may, in Mycroft's phrase, 'hear of Sherlock everywhere'; but there is no desire to see the record extended to the insignificant or the trivial. One noble gesture is nevertheless owed by the London County Council. In a letter to *The Times* in 1950 I suggested that they should install a plaque at No. 2 Devonshire Place in honour of Sir Arthur Conan Doyle having written the first Sherlock Holmes short stories there as he sat in his newly-opened consulting rooms awaiting his first patient. The centenary year must make this a reality.

The Sherlock Holmes Society's annual dinners are held in January at the Charing Cross Hotel. (It will be recalled that in a waiting room of this station Holmes had his left canine knocked out by Mathews. Nothing more is known of this redoubtable gentleman; but his achievement is a sufficient testimony — as permanent in its way as a plaque). On these occasions members are often invited to wear or carry something which identifies them with a character or incident in the saga, and fellow-diners at the hotel may thus have been startled to see an official of the Guildhall wearing the red fez cap of Culverton Smith, an

23

officer of the National Trust belted with the duelling rapier of Isadora Persano, or Gavin and Barbara Brend sporting the Cunningham tartan (their middle name) and carrying the odd and even words of the message from *The Reigate Squires*.

On one occasion when my wife was elegantly gowned and bustled as '*the* woman', I wore the baggy frockcoat, stock, and plaid trousers of the old pawnbroker in *The Red-headed League* — the ensemble being fittingly crowned by a flaming mass of carrotty hair. 'Good God', exclaimed one of the members, 'Who are you — Brendan Bracken?' On another night a distinguished surgeon in the society turned up as Dr Grimesby Roylott. As he was going home after garaging his car in Harley Street two girls encountered this apparition, heavily grease-painted, fiercely moustached and flourishing a riding crop. They stared: he leered: they shrieked — and fled.

The devotee of Holmes and Watson naturally accumulates books. John Murray has done sound service in providing all the stories in two omnibus volumes for the past 30 years; but they are not illustrated. The publisher should rise to his responsibilities. He could put the whole world in his debt by producing a new definitive edition, fully illustrated and fully annotated. For without the drawings, as I shall show in a later chapter, we lose something of the full savour of the saga. The *Strand* magazines, then, — and preferably in their original blue-green covers — are a 'must' for those who would make the true pilgrimage to Baker Street. I warn them that the quest is hard. Indeed, if they eventually find that volume of 1917 containing *His Last Bow* they may feel, as Holmes once felt, that their career has reached its summit.

Some of the earlier items are just as rare. For example, despite repeated appeals and advertisements, the Festival Year Exhibition had to open without a copy of the Beeton Annual which contains *A Study in Scarlet*. Eventually the Marylebone Library authorities were loaned a copy which the owner had picked up for sixpence. That is the best, perhaps almost the only, way of finding such gifts of fortune. My own adventures in this field have been both exciting and rewarding. It was on a fairly recent fourth of August ('as I have good reason to remember') that I found my copy of Beeton bound up with other paper-backs. Restraining a Watsonian impulse to cry 'Good heavens, Holmes, this is marvellous!', my mind went back to that earlier August when the two friends chatted in intimate converse on the terrace of Von Bork's house near Harwich. Full of years and honours as they were, and prophetic as was the speech of Holmes in that solemn epilogue, neither partner could have guessed that they would become ever more famous and that unborn, as well as untold, thousands would read and re-read their lightest word with the profoundest regard.

The Sherlockian interest is not easy to define. To some it is even tedious and I have occasionally detected heretical expressions which sounded dangerously like Watson's 'Ineffable twaddle' or Holmes' 'Unmitigated bleat'. But it is really too amiable a subject on which to quarrel and when I heard a well-known author suggest in public that it was regrettable that S. C. Roberts' 'dubious and childish' studies of Holmes should be allowed to get in the way of his true scholastic research on Dr Johnson, I naturally replied that it was indeed regrettable that dubious and childish research on Johnson should be allowed to inter-

fere with true scholarship in the study of Sherlock Holmes.
(I must interpolate here another Johnsonian quotation —
the scrap of dialogue, discovered by Chris. Morley,
between the Doctor and one of his friends who were com-
paring the sermons of various divines:

'Sir,' said he, 'do you ever read any others?'
'Yes, Doctor; I read Sherlock.'
'Ay, Sir, *there* you drink the cup of salvation to the bottom.')

Nor do I believe that there is any ground for the assumption that the Sherlockian cult exalts the character at the
expense of his creator. It is not that we love Conan Doyle
less, but that we love Sherlock Holmes more. Chris.
Morley, the founder of the Baker Street Irregulars of New
York indeed used to remark 'how ridiculous that the author
should only have been Knighted — he should have been
Sainted'. My old friend, the late Arthur Machen, once wrote:
'Why should we be interested in places more or less connected with the fortunes of people who never existed outside the brains and the pages of the romancers? I do not
know why we are thus interested, but I know that we are
so and that this interest constitutes one of the gentlest of
the pleasures of life' (*The London Adventure*).

The fellowship of Sherlock Holmes is certainly one of the
greatest as well as the gentlest pleasures of my own life and
I am grateful to author and character alike for continuing
delight and for friendships which reach across the world.
But I do not believe that a Conan Doyle Society, so named,
would have the same attraction. It has to be Sherlock
Holmes or nothing. And I am confident that the large and
genial author, notwithstanding his declared reservations
about his creation, would have chuckled at the idea. When

One Man's Pilgrimage

I think of Dr Jay Finley Christ, who gave me great gifts from his own collection, of Nathan Bengis who admitted me to membership of the Musgrave Ritualists of New York, of Russell McLaughlin who set me 'in good standing' with the Amateur Mendicants of Detroit, of A. D. Henriksen who put me on the role of the Sherlock Holmes Clubben of Denmark, or of Edgar Smith, the erudite editor of *The Baker Street Journal* — when I think of these representatives of the great host of aficionados everywhere, then I am more than half serious in believing that the Sherlockian interest (I had almost written 'faith') may have some minor but not unworthy part to play in furthering the ideal of wider international understanding.

But these are deep waters, Watson. When the Holborn Restaurant closed down I was able to buy a few glasses bearing its monogram and crest. There is no evidence that these are not the wine-glasses used by Watson and young Stamford when they lunched at the restaurant on that day-of-days in 1881. It is a great joy to me that some fellow Sherlockians are now able to raise these glasses when they 'look strangely over their wine' in honour of the Master. They will echo the song that the late Jim Montgomery, of Philadelphia, used to sing in what was surely the friendliest voice that ever came out of America:

> * O dear Sherlock, to share thy adventures we long,
> As you crush London's crime under heel,
> And we sing in thy praise an Irregular Song,
> Though it ne'er can express all we feel.
> Let grim warfare and pestilence rage as they can,
> You will still give long hours of joy
> To the boy who, adoring, is now half a man,
> Or the man who is yet half a boy.

* To the tune of 'Believe me if all those endearing young charms.'

27

How It All Began

Somewhere back in 1890 one or two unknown pioneers doubtless pondered over the singular fact that while *The Sign of Four* began on a day in July the month had become September by nightfall. And when the first short stories broke on the world in the ever-to-be-sanctified *Strand Magazine*, we may be sure that some acute reader would pick up the irregularity of Irene Adler's Lenten marriage at which Holmes was the sole witness, or attempt to reconcile the puzzling dates of Watson's sojourns in Baker Street.

These were the first whoever burst, the vanguard of the army of Baker Street Irregulars in all parts of the world who pore over the stories, not only for pure pleasure but also as an exercise in literary detection. Alas we do not know their names. They are as anonymous as the odd little procession of clients which flickers across the stage of 221B in the opening chapter of *A Study in Scarlet*. But those who bought the monthly *Strands* simply to enjoy the be-deer-stalkered detective's triumph over the latest devilry and those who hoped to find an additional bonus in the shape of some 'pretty little problem' of conflicting chronology belonged essentially to the same band. Both recognized that Holmes was something more than an ephemeral figure in a magazine: that he was here to stay.

How it All Began

If parody is the sincerest form of imitation, it seems clear that Holmes became a household name early in the famous *Strand* series. For in May, 1892, less than a year after the sequence had begun, Robert Barr wrote a capital burlesque for *The Idler* under the title 'The Adventures of Sherlaw Kombs'. It was followed in 1893 by a *Punch* series, 'The Adventures of Picklock Holes', by R. C. Lehmann. Both authors were happier in their imitations than in their pseudonyms, for Barr, who later published the admirable memoirs of the Continental detective, Eugene Valmont, wrote under the name of 'Luke Sharp' while Lehmann chose the equally elementary 'Cunnin Toil'. They were the forerunners of a long line of good-humoured travesties in which the great man variously appeared as Shamrock Jolnes, Herlock Sholmes, Holmlock Shears, Thinlock Bones, etc.

Young city men wore crepe round their hats when Holmes was apparently killed off by his creator in the last story of the *Memoirs*, but the editor of *Punch* was not in their ranks. In a footnote to the Lehmann series which concluded in the issue of December 30, 1893, he wrote with astonishing prescience:

'There is no proof positive given by an eye-witness whose veracity is unimpeachable of the death of the great amateur detective as it has been described in the *Strand Magazine* for this month. *Where is the merry Swiss boy who delivered the note and disappeared?* What was the symbolic meaning of the alpenstock with the hook at the end, left on the rock? Why, that he had *not* 'taken his hook'. Picklock Holes has disappeared, but so have a great many other people. That he will turn up again no student of detective history and of the annals of crime can possibly doubt. Is it

29

not probable that he has only dropped out of the *Strand Magazine*? And is it not equally probable that under some alias he will re-appear elsewhere? *Verb. sap.*'

Holmes was already passing into the national currency; was becoming as native as the weather, the Albert Hall, or grumbles about income tax or railway refreshment rooms. Even in the nineties he was being invoked in an advertisement for a famous brand of pills and named in catchy music hall songs. By 1902, Richard Harding Davis was able to introduce him into his novel *In the Fog* in such institutional terms as had hitherto been reserved for Pickwick or Falstaff:

'I would give a hundred pounds', he whispered, 'if I could place in his hands at this moment a new story of Sherlock Holmes — a thousand pounds,' he added wildly — 'five thousand pounds!'

It was in the latter year that Frank Sidgwick launched the first scientific study of the Sherlockian canon in the form of an open letter to Dr Watson in *The Cambridge Review*. This letter queried various inconsistencies in *The Hound of the Baskervilles*, then being serialized in the *Strand*. It concluded: 'Lastly and worst of all you cannot have been living with Sherlock in Baker Street at this date because in *The Sign of Four* you became engaged to Miss Mary Morstan in September 1888 and you were married a few months later. How then in October 1889 were you still a bachelor in Baker Street?' Sidgwick was a poet — I believe he once wrote a sonnet with only one word in each line — and became a publisher. He suspected a strain of minor poetry in Watson: a true judgment, for there are hints of verse, or near-verse, in several of the stories. This, for example, from *The Valley of Fear*:

How it All Began

> Do you say that no-one
> Can ever get level
> With this king-devil?

Or these from *The Three Garridebs*:

> You will find a chair here, Mr Holmes,
> Pray allow me to clear these bones.
>
> . . . .
>
> You spoke of some bones, Mr Mason
> Could you show them before you go?

(The latter quotation was quarried by Justin Clarke-Hall, the Sherlockian bookseller of Pope's — sorry — of Wine Office Court, opposite Dr Johnson's 'Cheshire Cheese'.)

Sir Gerald Kelly, former President of the Royal Academy, might indeed have become the Number One researcher in this field, for he has recorded that while at Cambridge around 1900 he discussed the inconsistencies of Jabez Wilson's narrative with M. R. James, the author of some of the most famous ghost stories in the world. But Monty James was unaccountably not very much interested and so, says Sir Gerald 'though I had the handle in my hand, I never turned it nor went through the door where other scholars had such interesting experiences'.

But if Cambridge blazed the trail, the late Mgr Ronald Knox may be said to have founded the Sherlockian school of higher criticism with his paper, 'Studies in the Literature of Sherlock Holmes', written at Oxford in 1911. In a long survey of the Baker Street saga he gravely questioned the Watsonian authenticity of certain episodes, discussed some of the difficulties of dating, and applied the terms of classic criticism to an analysis of structure and style. His aim, wrote Miss Dorothy Sayers in *Unpopular Opinions*, was to show that 'by these methods, one could disintegrate a

31

modern classic as speciously as a certain school of critics have endeavoured to disintegrate the Bible'.

The continuing appearance of the stories in the *Strand Magazine* until 1927 together with plays, films and numerous reprintings in book form were all built into the fabric of the Sherlock Holmes legend. (It is a point for the curious that what is perhaps Holmes' most quoted phrase 'Elementary, my dear Watson,' does not in fact appear in any story. There are several isolated 'Elementaries' and 'My dear Watsons', but nowhere are they combined.)

The purely Sherlockian movement can, however, be dated from 1928; for that year brought the first omnibus volume of the short stories from John Murray and the publication of Mgr Knox's earlier study in his collected *Essays in Satire*. Together they sparked off a number of notable reviews in a similarly dead-pan approach and so the game was set firmly afoot. These early collectors' pieces included S. C. Roberts' reply to Mgr Knox (*Cambridge Review 1928*), Ivar Gunn's 'Examination Paper on Sherlock Holmes' (*Life and Letters*, December, 1928) and A. A. Milne's 'Dr Watson Speaks Out' (reproduced in the author's *By Way of Introduction*).

The publication of the omnibus of the four long stories by Murray in 1929 and the revival of the Gillette play in the winter of that year helped to fan the Holmesian flame. So did the world-wide tributes which marked the death of Sir Arthur Conan Doyle in 1930, even though they brought the lamentable realization that there could be no more glimpses through the magic door of 221B.

The Sherlockian movement was solidly based, however, and soon came a succession of detailed foundational studies: S. C. Roberts' biography of Dr Watson in 1931,

How it All Began

Sherlock Holmes and Dr Watson: A chronology of their Adventures by the late H. W. Bell and *Sherlock Holmes: Fact or Fiction?* by T. S. Blakeney, both in 1932, and Vincent Starrett's *Private Life of Sherlock Holmes* in 1934. The latter year also saw the development of Sherlockian sodalities — the founding of the Baker Street Irregulars of New York and the setting up of the Sherlock Holmes Society in London which dined annually and appropriately in Baker Street but unaccountably on Derby night. I shall not attempt to summarize the many ingenious theories by which these distinguished savants sought to resolve the apparent irreconcilables in the chronology, but if you can obtain copies of their books you will have what has been called 'the best winter evening reading of a life time'.

The Sherlockian cult of course has its conventions. Holmes and Watson are regarded as real people. The stories are assumed to have been written by John H. Watson, M.D., late of the Indian Army. In the extreme American view, Conan Doyle is simply the literary agent who introduced Watson to his publisher. I do not think our friends across the Atlantic are very well found in their fond allusion to Sir Arthur as 'the literary agent'. After all, it is in his personal record that he sold Dr Watson's first reminiscences outright for a mere £25 — an appallingly bad bargain which would have ensured his expulsion from any gathering of literary agents anywhere!

An American might have become a Big Elk or a Tall Cedar of Lebanon in pre-Sherlockian days; and such resounding titles as the Speckled Band of Boston, the Hounds of the Baskerville of Chicago, the Creeping Men of Cleveland and the Wisteria Lodge Confederates of the Eastern Deep South indicate that the flair for picturesque clubbery is well sustained. Nearly forty societies now keep green the memory in U.S.A. alone. The head of the Baker Street Irregulars raps for order with a gavel made from the doorway of a blitzed house in Baker Street; the Musgrave Ritualists of New York chant a Latin version of the sacred formula; the Dancing Men of Providence have a sundial at their meetings on which appropriate cypher messages are secured by a pebble; in others there are ritual toasts and observances. Meetings commonly open with a random quiz and anyone faulted is liable to buy a round of drinks from the group of 'ancient and cobwebby bottles' on the sideboard. Members are apt to turn up in hansom cabs or deerstalkers. Chris Morley invented a tie of blue, purple and mouse-colour stripes to commemorate the three shades of the Master's dressing gowns. After dinner, papers are read and new theories expounded.

In this recreative detection, much of the zest undoubtedly stems from the waywardness of Watson. Although he once told Holmes that he had all the facts in his journal and that the public should know them, his chronology and chronicling are at times so imprecise that we begin to believe that he must have either transcribed his notes too hurriedly or read them imperfectly. Thus the exact date of Holmes' birth, his university and the location of his bee farm in Sussex are still matters for discussion. Nor, as may be seen in a later chapter, has the nimbus of Baker Street fog around the true original of 221B been wholly dispersed. As for Watson himself, the period of his various practices, the number of his wives and his wounds, the duration of the many events which separate Maiwand from Marylebone — such desiderata are among the most baffling problems in the canon.

34

It is the aim of the Sherlockian world to reconcile such irregularities. Yet who can say the westward land is bright? S. C. Roberts noted in 1931 'the growing agreement among scholars as to the year of Watson's marriage to Miss Mary Morstan'; but when the latest of the six major chronologies was published in 1955 it was apparent that perfect unanimity had been achieved on the dating of only a handful of the sixty stories in the canon. Again, although 1954 was informally agreed as the centenary date of Holmes' birth, the critical estimates have ranged between 1952 and 1959.

But to try and be a Sherlockian is to find that Conan Doyle keeps breaking in, and there are those who set down the discrepancies of dating merely to the speed with which the author rattled off the stories for the *Strand*. Conan Doyle naturally breaks in in other, larger, ways. For when Holmes forgives the offenders in such stories as *The Cardboard Box* and *The Blue Carbuncle* we are vividly reminded of the same high sense of justice which moved Sir Arthur to engage in lone and costly fights for the vindication of Oscar Slater and George Edalji; and when we read that Watson refused to fire on the unarmed convict on Dartmoor, the words are those of J. H. W., but the chivalrous sentiment behind them is that of A. C. D. himself.

The rigour of the Sherlockian game consists in indulging legitimate speculation regarding the lives of Holmes and Watson, in evolving new theories from existing evidence, and, not least, in catching out the other fellow. Thus, when S. C. Roberts incautiously hinted that John H. Watson's mother might have had Tractarian leanings and named her son 'John Henry' after Newman, the late H. W. Bell rejected the theory as improbable since

Newman had joined the Roman church several years before the putative date of Watson's birth. And when Gavin
Brend, himself an old Westminster boy, put forward a
theory that Holmes' exact knowledge of all the streets in
that area might mean that he also had been a scholar
there, someone retorted that the same topographical sign-
posts could equally demonstrate that Holmes had attended
the Grey Coat School, or even the Board School, in the
same neighbourhood. I am chastened when I think of the
pocket lenses which may be turned on these pages, the dis-
putatious cherry-woods that may be waved and the deerstalker caps thrown gleefully in the air when the scrutineers
pounce on the inevitable error.

Miss Sayers believed that the Sherlockian exercise 'must
be played as solemnly as a county cricket match at Lord's:
the slightest touch of extravagance or burlesque ruins the
atmosphere'. Myself, I would draw the line less rigidly,
since some of the most fantastic theories are also among the
most ingenious. Rex Stout, the American detective-story
writer, startled the Baker Street Irregulars a few years ago
by the outrageously heretical suggestion that Watson was
a woman. Among much supporting evidence, he produced
an acrostic from the titles of selected stories in which the
initial upright was made to read 'IRENE WATSON'. Dr
Julian Wolff, a fellow Irregular, thereupon replied with an
equally cunning acrostic, also compiled from the story
titles, in which the diagonal spelled out: 'NUTS TO REX
STOUT.' Your true Sherlockian makes it a point of honour
to reply in kind and I am reminded that when the late
Ivar Gunn received a letter in 'Dancing Men' symbols he
immediately responded in 'Gloria Scott' code.

In these days when the tempo runs to ulcers rather than

to ulsters, there is much comfort in the apparent inexhaustibility of the Sherlockian seam. Nor will the game lack its distinguished devotees. They range from Bernard Darwin, a Fundamentalist who sturdily refuses to dabble in dates and stands by every story as published in order due, to Dr Jay Finley Christ, formerly of the University of Chicago, whose concordance, of monumental patience and value, indexes the principal subject under S instead of H on the correct 221B precedent. Meanwhile another American, Pope R. Hill, Sr, of Athens, Georgia, has recently elaborated an arresting theory that each story in the saga contains a hidden alternative solution whose acceptance is claimed to resolve all existing inconsistencies. One can only echo the Master's words to Lestrade in the *Hound*: 'The biggest thing for years.'

Sidney Paget's Drawings

Sherlock Holmes is most familiarly known by his deer-stalker hat and curved pipe. Yet neither of these accessories is named anywhere in the official saga. They are the invention, or shall we say the inspiration, of his most famous illustrators. Sidney Paget, of London, produced the deerstalker and Frederic Dorr Steele, of New York, the curved pipe.

Moreover, if Paget had not had an artist brother, the Holmes of tradition might have been a very different character; might, indeed, have been the figure his creator intended him to be. In *Memories and Adventures* Conan Doyle wrote of Holmes: 'He had, as I imagined him, a thin razor-like face with a great hawks-bill of a nose, and two small eyes, set close together on either side of it. It chanced, however, that Sidney Paget had a younger brother who served him as a model. The handsome Walter took the place of the more powerful, but uglier, Sherlock, and perhaps from the point of view of my lady readers it was as well.'

It is worth noticing that Holmes also lost height in the Paget metamorphosis. Conan Doyle saw his detective as 'rather over six feet, and so excessively lean that he appeared to be considerably taller'. Yet I doubt whether he ever appears to be more than 5 feet 10 inches in the

Strand Magazine. Indeed, in Paget's Regent Street drawing he is shown as exactly the same height as Watson. A giant, nevertheless.

And here is another point. Do we not tend to think of Holmes as middle-aged in our mental picture? What a shock, then, to realize that he could only have been about twenty-seven when he and Watson went into partnership at 221B. Yet why should Holmes' youthfulness surprise us? Conan Doyle himself was exactly the same age when Holmes made his first bow in the manuscript of *A Study in Scarlet*.

Sidney Paget was not the first of the illustrators: only the best. The first was D. H. Friston who, in the scarce 'Beeton' edition of *A Study in Scarlet*, incredibly depicted Holmes with side-blinds and billycock hat. The second artist was Doyle père whom the author described as 'more terrible than Blake'. Another early illustrator gave the detective a braided jacket and a curly-brimmed bowler. It was left to Paget to fix him for all time in the pages of the old *Strand Magazine*.

From the opening episode of the *Adventures* in 1891 to the close of the *Return* series in 1904, Paget drew some 350 illustrations for the saga — a wide-ranging gallery through which the famous profile gradually etched itself upon the affections of the whole world.

One of Paget's most brilliant touches was undoubtedly the deerstalker hat. It made its first appearance when Holmes and Watson were travelling down to Boscombe Valley and was merely based on the description of Holmes wearing his 'long grey travelling cloak and close-fitting cloth cap'. In an article in 1950 I argued that there were other kinds of contemporary headgear which would have fitted such a description. For example, in an early issue of the *Strand Magazine*, Conan Doyle was photographed astride a fearsome tandem tricycle wearing a small round hat of of the type known as a cricket cap. A famous hatter was also advertising a pocket travelling hat at that time: 'They fall into two or three negligé shapes at the will of the wearer. These hats are *luxuriously lined with Real Russian Leather*, the aroma of which is lasting and delightfully refreshing.' Either of these varieties might have been described as a 'close-fitting cloth cap'. Conan Doyle dutifully accepted the artist's invention, however, for in the *Silver Blaze* story which appeared about a year after Paget had first introduced the deerstalker, Holmes' sharp, eager face was described as 'framed in his ear-flapped travelling cap'.

The curious incident of the deerstalker was cleared up by Miss Winifred Paget, the artist's daughter, in the first number of *The Sherlock Holmes Journal* in 1952 when she revealed that her father, living much in the country, wore a deerstalker himself and transferred it to Holmes just as he transferred to Watson in *The Hound of the Baskervilles* the rural knickerbockers similarly worn by his friend Alfred Morris Butler.

Although Paget used the deerstalker sparingly in the *Strand Magazine*, it has persisted as the traditional headgear of the Master. It set the key for William Gillette's striking impersonation on the stages of U.S.A. and this country at the turn of the century; and when the last of the stories appeared in the *Strand* in 1927 the illustrator, Frank Wiles, gave Holmes a deerstalker in graceful compliment to its only begetter. More recently, the deerstalker has been flourished across the sumptuous coloured illustrations by Robert Fawcett for the series of *Exploits* by Adrian Conan Doyle and John Dickson Carr.

No less permanent in the Baker Street gallery are Paget's drawings of Dr Watson who, as the late Mgr Ronald Knox commented, 'above all things else stands exalted in history as the wearer of the unconquerable bowler hat.' True, Watson may sometimes be shown professionally in a silk hat or mouching about Dartmoor in a peaked cap (and the borrowed knickerbockers!) but it is to the bowler hat that memory fondly and finally returns.

To Sidney Paget we owe some of the most thrilling glimpses of the partners in action. Who can forget the scene in the mist as the hell-hound, wreathed in flame, bursts upon them; the shadowy eeriness of the room in which, with lamp and pistol at the ready, they find the victim of the Speckled Band; the pin-drop tension of their vigil in the Empty House as they lie in wait for 'the most cunning and dangerous criminal in London'?

Memorable, too, are the numerous drawings of the cosy sitting-room at 221B with the armchair, never quite deep enough, one feels, to accommodate the coiled length of the detective; the breakfast table with its ample snowy cloth, just now, perhaps, bearing the dish which conceals the precious Naval Treaty; even the door whose hinges are so endearingly uncertain, opening now left, now right.

Although much detail is given there are significant omissions. For example, the Persian slipper which held Holmes' tobacco is never shown; nor the jack-knife with which he transfixed unanswered correspondence to the mantelshelf. One could also wish that Paget had left us some photograph, however fugitive, of Mrs Hudson, the indomitable landlady of 221B. I for one have always regretted that he made so few drawings of outdoor London. Less than a dozen, in fact. There are only two illustrations of the outside of 221B — one in *A Scandal in Bohemia*, the other in *The Empty House*. And these do not agree as the fanlight is semi-circular in the first-named and square-headed in the other. Yet when one remembers how magnificently Paget could delineate the London street-scene in such a drawing as that of Holmes and Watson in Regent Street, one would willingly exchange a few of the character sketches — Holmes in disguise, for example — for a sight of, say, Watson in Wigmore Street, the afternoon walk through the Park, or the saunter along the Baker Street of the nineties in the wake of Sir Henry Baskerville and Dr Mortimer.

Sidney Paget registered other achievements — exhibited pictures in the Royal Academy, illustrated non-Holmesian stories for the *Strand* and painted portraits which are still to be found on the walls of public buildings in London and elsewhere. (One is at Mill Hill School and others are in Finsbury and Paddington Town Halls.) Yet one feels that these were merely asides to his essential work of recording the exploits of the most famous of all detectives.

Paget naturally limned the age in which he lived so that the sitting room at 221B became a microcosm of the leisurely, secure and utterly vanished London world of hansoms and foggy gas-lit streets of the nineties. That, doubtless, is the clue to the evocative and undiminishing appeal of the drawings. As one turns the old pages of the *Strand*, wheels grind on the kerb, the bell rings, pulses quicken at the sound of a step on the stair. At one moment the doorway frames the fantastic figure of the King of

Bohemia; at another the huge negro bruiser, Steve Dixie ('Which of you genelmen is Masser Holmes?'); at a third the ponderous piece of wreckage from the Priory School. No matter whom. For us, as for Holmes and Watson, the stage is set, the hunt is up, and, in their own favourite phrase, the game is afoot.

Sidney Paget died in 1908; Conan Doyle in 1930. The old *Strand Magazine* itself folded up in 1950 in its sixtieth year. But 'Holmes and Watson', says Vincent Starret, one of their distinguished American admirers, 'still live for all that love them well: in a romantic chamber of the heart: in a nostalgic country of the mind: where it is always 1895.' And one may be sure that on a peg in a corner of that snug, romantic chamber, somewhere near the violin and the hunting crop, hang — just as Sidney Paget drew them — those twin symbols of immortality, the deerstalker and the bowler hat.

Dorr Steele and Some Others

Like Sidney Paget, Frederic Dorr Steele modelled his drawings of Holmes on a real person. Steele's original was William Gillette, the American actor who wrote and played the name-part in a powerful melodrama which opened at the Lyceum Theatre, London, in 1901 after a successful run in the United States.

Gillette made a handsome detective and with his deer-stalker, riding crop and curved pipe helped to establish the legend even more firmly. The play, however, was largely Gillette's invention, despite the introduction of Moriarty and other characters; and, good theatre though it was, the Sherlockians of the day must have shuddered to see the Master embracing the young heroine at the final curtain. So callous was Conan Doyle to their suscepti-bilities that he wired to Gillette: 'You may marry or murder or do what you like with him.' Yet when Beverley Nichols suggested the same thing in an interview with Conan Doyle in the 1920's, the reply was: 'You can't bring love affairs into detective stories. As soon as you begin to make your detective too human, the story flops. It falls to the ground. You have to be ruthlessly analytical about the whole thing. If I had made Holmes human. . . .'

George Newnes showed sound business instinct by bringing out a special 'souvenir' edition of the Holmes stories and advertising it in the theatre programme during the run. A burlesque entitled 'Sheerluck Jones' was also put on at Terry's Theatre. The scale of parody may be judged from the circumstance that Holmes' hypodermic needle was represented by a garden syringe. To have had the original and the parody running at the same time must have been unique in London theatre history. No firmer testimony to the epic stature of Holmes could be imagined.

Steele was a fine incisive draughtsman and many of his drawings are in the true spirit of the period. But he was somewhat wayward on detail. The thumbprint on the wall in *The Norwood Builder*, for example, becomes a complete 'red hand' in his drawing. He, or perhaps his publishers, also confused the text by using the same drawing in more than one story under different captions. It could also be a criticism that Steele's detective, like his original, was a trifle too elegant, too debonair. He belonged to the drawing room. One could scarcely picture him full-length in the dust of the empty house at Lauriston Gardens, Brixton, reading the riddle of Patent-leathers and Square-toes through his 'large, round magnifying glass'. Steele nevertheless remains one of the very best, as well as one of the most prolific, illustrators of the saga. He also gave us one tantalizingly brief glimpse of Mrs Hudson.

George Hutchison, whose 40 illustrations for *A Study in Scarlet* ran through many editions from 1891 onwards, never appeared to be at ease with the Master. The unhappy key was set by the drawing of the famous introduction at Barts in which Watson and young Stamford could have been a couple of shaggy characters from *The Diary of a Nobody*. Apart from the depiction of the struggle with Jefferson Hope (always enormously enhanced for me by

45

the caption: 'They sprang upon him like so many stag-hounds,') too many of the drawings verged on the crude or the faintly comic. And in the illustration in which Holmes tracks the old woman visitor along Baker Street, the artist contrived a triple inaccuracy, not to mention equipping Holmes with a bowler hat. The scene is shown to be in daylight, although it occurred at 'close on nine' on an evening of early March; even if daylight is allowed as artistic licence, the shadows wrongly fall from east to west instead of from west to east; and finally Holmes hides behind a high garden wall of a kind which never existed in Baker Street.

Yet Hutchinson was no ham-fisted amateur. He made excellent drawings for at least one other of Conan Doyle's books and was a regular contributor to Ward Lock's *Windsor Magazine* and Jerome K. Jerome's *Idler*. Indeed, it is ironical that his illustrations for a Holmesian burlesque in the latter periodical in 1892 were wholly admirable, several being modelled on Sidney Paget's drawings which had of course begun to appear in the *Strand* the previous year.

One fancies that some kind of goblin must have snarled up the early history of this first book about Sherlock, for as well as being unlucky in its illustrators, the MSS had gone the rounds, read and unread, and had finally been disposed of at a give-away price. The gremlin influence persisted after publication. For one in whom the dramatic instinct was remarkably developed, Holmes' first bow could not be regarded as outstanding. Beeton's shilling Christmas Annual provided the shaky stage; even so, he had to share it with the text of two pawky drawing-room sketches; one of the characters bore the name of Miss

46

Tetbury Tattleton. D. H. Friston's four drawings depicted an alien Holmes, a hang-dog moustachioed Watson, and a Lestrade and Gregson who appear to be all the Master said of them. (Friston illustrated J. S. le Fanu's vampire story *Carmilla* in 1871/2. I should like to see those drawings.)

If we allow for the natural sentiment which surrounds a firstling, especially one born so precariously, we shall doubtless admit that Friston's drawings were less than ideal. But at least they were bolder than the curious and colourless line drawings which Charles Doyle, the author's father, drew for the second edition. I have a copy of *Our Trip to Blunderland* illustrated by the same artist ten years earlier. These sketches are much sharper, just as quaint, but of course twice as successful. One suspects that some of the Sherlockian delineations, notably the group of Baker Street Irregulars, might have had their origins in this earlier set of drawings.

It was not, however, until James Greig took a hand in the mid-nineties that *A Study in Scarlet* was at all worthily illustrated. Greig produced eight drawings, not uniformly successful, for a special give-away edition which formed a supplement to the Christmas Number of the *Windsor Magazine* of 1895. The paper cover of this collector's piece bears a strong design in colour, a study in *rouge et noir* indeed. That volume of the *Windsor* should be admitted to one's collection for another reason: it contains illustrations to non-Sherlockian stories by Hutchinson, Greig and F. H. Townsend.

It was in 1903 that Townsend made a single but memorable contribution to the saga with eight drawings for *The Sign of Four*. Alec Twidle, who also illustrated later stories in the *Strand*, contributed special illustrations for the dignified 'author's edition' published by John Murray in the same year. Both artists were clearly enthusiastic in their work. It is instructive to compare their treatment of Holmes or of the fate of the Andaman islander in *The Sign of Four* — both equally compelling and both singularly alike.

Sidney Paget's noble series of drawings for the *Strand* ended with *The Return* in 1904 and it fell to Twidle, H. M. Brock, Howard Elcock, Alfred Gilbert and others to continue the tradition in the remaining adventures which appeared intermittently until 1927. These later stories were subsequently reprinted under the titles of *His Last Bow* and *The Case Book*. The last of the four long stories, *The Valley of Fear*, was also published serially in the *Strand* during the first World War with masterly drawings by Frank Wiles.

There are still a few seniors among us who had the good fortune, the miraculously good fortune, to read the *Adventures* and the *Memoirs* as they first appeared between the blue-green covers of the old *Strand* in the early eighteen-nineties. That pleasure can be tasted at second-hand — literally at second-hand — since those early bound volumes are still blessedly numerous. Paradoxically, it is the later *Strands*, from, say, 1910 to 1927, which are really scarce. The magazine and its readers had both changed with the years. By the nineteen-twenties the magazine had become virtually a string of short stories. It was still widely read; but on train journeys rather than in bound volumes.

One might trace the gradual emergence of Holmes to world eminence through the illustrations in the old files of the *Strand*. In the *Adventures* and *Memoirs* series of short stories in the early nineties, he was not always given first

2 The Regent Street along which Holmes and Watson strolled in *The Hound of the Baskervilles*

3 Wyndham Robinson's whimsical evocation of some of the early Sidney Paget drawings

place in the magazine. Only once, and this was in the last story of the *Memoirs*, was he honoured by a full-page drawing. The story was, of course, *The Final Problem*. Sidney Paget's spirited illustration showed Holmes locked in the arms of Moriarty on the edge of the Reichenbach Falls and blandly gave away the secret with the caption 'The Death of Sherlock Holmes'.

A full page drawing at the opening of each episode was well established in the serial appearance of the *Hound* in 1901–2 and in the *Return* stories the following year. After that, the illustrations were sometimes given a double page. These later adventures were also well advertised in advance in the magazine. In browsing over these old magazines some time ago I thought for a wild moment that I had discovered a new adventure. In the issue of February 1927, a forthcoming story was announced as *The Adventure of the Black Spaniel*. When the story eventually appeared, however, it carried the title of *Shoscombe Old Place*, the name by which it is known today. In passing, I remember references in the *Sherlock Holmes Journal* to legends of ghost dogs in various parts of the country besides Dartmoor. One of these spoke of a spaniel haunting the Isle of Man. One nevertheless felt that such a beast, supernatural or not, could scarcely measure up to the Baskerville monster. 'Mr Holmes, they were the footprints of a gigantic — spaniel'!

In the Sherlock Holmes series there are 56 short stories and only four long narratives. Conan Doyle believed that some part of the success of the Holmes short stories was due to his invention of the complete-in-itself episode as an alternative to the customary serial story. He logically claimed that interest in the serial was lost if a single instalment was missed, whereas the short story series would always stand up individually.

For those of us who were not sufficiently fortunate to be able to read the original *Strands* the delineations of Holmes' middle and late periods are equally nostalgic. The deer-stalker disappears. In Paget's drawings it makes its last bow in *Black Peter* — a drawing in which Inspector Stanley Hopkins incidentally looks remarkably like Lord Attlee. Holmes and Watson change little with the passage of years, save that Holmes' hair recedes somewhat from the temples. Yet in these drawings from the *Strands* of 1914 onwards they tend to glide imperceptibly nearer to our own period in their clothing and general background. So we have the contradiction that while they belong inescapably to the nineties we are to some extent conditioned by the illustrations to accept the eventual telephone at 221B and even the motor-car which Watson drives in 1914. A conspectus of Sherlockian illustrations, together with much illuminating material, was given in the late James Montgomery's *A Study in Pictures* published in Philadelphia as his *Christmas Annual* in 1954.

It would be impossible to record the innumerable other artists, major and minor, who have paid their tribute of affection to Sherlock Holmes over the years. But I should like to single out the unknown artist who introduced the Master into an advertisement for Beecham's pills in the early nineties; and the illustrator who presented a new character to 221B by drawing a cat by the side of Holmes' armchair in the frontispiece of the Nelson pocket edition of the *Adventures*. A most elegant Holmes in figured dressing gown, winged collar and black stock with scarf-pin, was contributed to *Vanity Fair* by 'Spy' at the time of the

Gillette play's run in London. Nor should one omit the fine cartoon of Holmes and Conan Doyle by Sir Bernard Partridge which originally appeared in *Punch* in 1926 and is now becomingly housed in the National Portrait Gallery. This telling drawing, which shows the giant author with his head in the clouds chained by the ankles to a diminutive Holmes, is apparently based on Sir Arthur's famous (or infamous?) remark: 'He takes my mind from better things.'

Above all, I must mention the virtually unknown artist who designed the front cover of the old *Strand* magazine. For me, as for countless thousands the world over, this was the first magical vision of London. Especially the coloured covers of those 'Grand Christmas Double Numbers' with snow lying like icing on the old-fashioned street lamps and shop-fronts, the hansoms and horse-buses skidding across the frozen thoroughfare, the newsboy with the vivid green cover of *Titbits* showing under his arm, the prominence of the advertisements for Fry's cocoa, and over all, against a leaden sky, the proud steeples of St Mary-le-Strand and St Clement Danes looking down upon a seasonable shopping scene of almost Dickensian bustle and bonhomie, not yet dispersed by the ordered impersonality of the Aldwych widening scheme.

Yes, that was the beckoning London which the artist created. His name, I can tell you, was G. Haite, and he drew about twenty sketches before old Sir George Newnes was satisfied. 'In time to come,' said Sir George, 'I should like the cover of the *Strand* to become as familiar to the mind of the public as is the cover of *Punch*.' There can be no doubt that the hope was fulfilled; for, apart from the substitution of motor vehicles for hansoms and horse buses around 1913, the cover scene remained virtually unchanged from 1891 until World War Two.

As a footnote one may recall that Newnes originally thought of naming the new publication the *Burleigh Street Magazine* or the *New Magazine*. Within whose pages our team of artists might not inappropriately have depicted the adventures of Mr Sherrinford Holmes and Dr Ormond Sacker!

Where Was 221B?

One of the perennial problems for the student of the Holmes saga is to try and locate the original of 221B, Baker Street. Some American irregulars have lately attempted to show that Mrs Hudson's famous boarding house was not in Baker Street at all, but in the parallel street called Gloucester Place. They claim that this was a device of Watson's to protect Holmes from the Moriarty gang and that Gloucester Place anyway looks much more like the Baker Street of tradition than the present-day Baker Street of gown shops and milk bars. But surely the legend is destroyed if 221B is divorced from Baker Street? It seems to me that if you put it in Gloucester Place you might just as well put it in Charing Cross Road.

In any case Gloucester Place does not fit in with the main clue to the identity of 221B given in *The Empty House*. It will be recalled that this house, where Holmes and Watson lay in wait for Colonel Moran and his deadly airgun, was known as Camden House, was opposite their old quarters, and that the approach was described by Watson with considerable detail:

'We emerged at last into a small road, lined with old, gloomy houses, which led us into Manchester Street, and so to Blandford Street. Here we turned swiftly down a narrow passage, passed through a wooden gate into a deserted yard, and then opened with a key the back door of a house.'

It is generally accepted that 221B was on the west side of Baker Street in accordance with the directions quoted above. An awkward point is, however, raised in *The Cardboard Box* where the wall of the house *opposite* 221B has the morning sun shining on it. A possible explanation is that the sitting-room at 221B might have had a third window at the opposite side of the room to the two opening on to Baker Street. This third window would look out onto houses at the back of 221B and Watson could have glanced out of it and correctly noted the sun-glare on a wall facing east. A rear window of this kind is hinted in at least one of Sidney Paget's drawings and is specifically indicated in Mr Ernest Short's plan of the rooms which appeared in the final issue of the *Strand* in March 1950. On the other hand, I have suggested in the last chapter of this book that Watson may not have been feeling very well on that hot August morning and was thus somewhat confused in recollection. The glare which upset him might simply have been the direct morning sunshine streaming through the Baker Street windows and that when he later wrote down the scene he mistakenly referred to reflected sunlight.

But if there is broad agreement that the house was on the west side of the street, there are numerous theories regarding the exact location. These variously place it (*a*) on the present site of Abbey House (between Regent's Park and Marylebone Road); (*b*) or as either Nos. 109 or 111 (between Marylebone Road and York Street); (*c*) or somewhere in the blocks immediately north or south of Blandford Street (Nos. 45–67 or 19–35). How reassuring it would be in this Conan Doyle centenary year if the precise position of 221B could be established, like good old Watson himself, as 'the one fixed point in a changing age'.

Let us examine the evidence.

The principal claim for Abbey House, the headquarters of the Abbey Road Building Society, is that it occupies Nos. 219–223 Baker Street. An early article in the society's magazine recalled that this part of the street was originally known as Upper Baker Street and showed that on the page of Conan Doyle's note-book in which the first thoughts about Holmes and Watson were jotted down, the address appeared as 221B *Upper* Baker Street. I don't attach any importance to the fact that Abbey House chances to bestride the original number; for Conan Doyle (or should one say John H. Watson?) conventionally used fictitious numbers while naming real streets. Examples are No. 403 Brook Street (*The Resident Patient*) and No. 427 Park Lane (*The Empty House*). Nor, remembering that the author's topography was not always impeccable, should any significance be allowed to the '*Upper* Baker Street' note. Indeed, I believe that this reference really meant no more than the *upper part* of Baker Street: i.e. not the lower part around Portman Square. Just how little weight should be given to this point may be judged from the fact that in Conan Doyle's stage version of *The Speckled Band* the scene of action is described on one page as 'Mr Sherlock Holmes' Rooms, *Upper* Baker Street, London', and on another as 'Mr Sherlock Holmes' room in Baker Street'.

But there are at least two further considerations which, to my mind, completely discount the validity of the Abbey House claim. The first is that since Abbey House is virtually opposite one entrance to Baker Street Station, Watson could scarcely have described the distracted banker (*The Beryl Coronet*) as 'approaching from the direction of the Metropolitan Station' if 221B had been on this site. The other, and weightier point, is that as Marylebone Road is the widest and most important thoroughfare in the whole area, Watson could not have failed both to recognize and name it if they had in fact crossed it to reach the empty house; and that anyway it cannot be squared with the description of the approach along the narrow passage from Blandford Street.

Before examining the respective claims of the two remaining groups, i.e. Nos. 109/111 and 19/35–45/67, some minor points must be disposed of. The first of these is concerned with Watson's visit to the Wigmore Street Post Office in *The Sign of Four*. (Holmes, you will recall, guessed that Watson had called there because the pavement was up outside the building and he saw that his partner's instep bore traces of reddish brown earth. Incidentally one of my friends made the profoundly disturbing discovery that the soil at that point is black, not red!)

Those who maintain that Nos. 109/111 are not the true site of 221B point out that Watson would not be likely to go as far as Wigmore Street when there were two alternative post offices much nearer home — one at No. 45 Upper Baker Street, the other a few doors above Blandford Street. To this I reply that there is no indication that Watson used the nearest post office on that occasion. Indeed, as Holmes appears to have been in a somewhat exasperating mood that morning, it would be reasonable to suppose that the good doctor had gone for a pre-luncheon stroll and had called at Wigmore Street in passing. He states explicitly that his visit to the post office was 'a sudden impulse'.

Enthusiasts should be grateful that this familiar landmark has come down to us in its best-known form. Wigmore Street was known at the period of the adventure as 'Upper Seymour Street' and the earliest editions of *The Sign of Four* refer to it as 'the Seymour Street office'. Obviously the place where Ormond Sacker would have conducted his postal business! In passing, Holmes made no more than a lucky guess in supposing that Watson had sent a wire from the post office. Watson might have called there to consult the post office directory, to inquire about the rates for letters to Afghanistan or Ballarat, or even to renew the licence for the bull-pup which he had doubtless had to board out since *A Study in Scarlet* days.

In *My dear Holmes* Gavin Brend suggested that Nos. 109/111 are so close to Baker Street Station that Alexander Holder, the banker, would never have contemplated taking a cab on that snowy February morning when he came to tell the story of the beryl coronet. I submit that he never intended to take a cab from Baker Street Station to 221B. When he arrived there, quite out of breath, he told Holmes: 'I came to Baker Street by the Underground, and hurried from there on foot, for the cabs go slowly through this snow.' Now Mr Holder lived at Streatham and as Holmes and Watson later went back with him by train he presumably came up by the same means, probably arriving at Victoria Station. From this point an inveterate cabtaker would surely have engaged a hansom or four-wheeler to 221B — had the weather been normal. Mr Holder was so distracted on arriving at 221B that he may have been forgiven a slight incoherence. I believe that what he really meant to convey to Holmes was: 'I came to Baker Street by the Underground — for the cabs go slowly through this snow — and hurried from there on foot.' In other words, he had utterly dismissed cabs as practicable means of transport because of the snow. Note in support of this suggestion that somewhat later in the day our taker-of-very-little-exercise leads Holmes and Watson *on foot* from Streatham Station to his home.

It has also been contended that since the banker was 'running hard' when Watson saw him from the sitting-room window, 221B must have been a considerable distance from the station — too far, in fact, for Nos. 109/111 to merit consideration. I believe that the distance from the station to these two houses, short as it is, would have been quite sufficient to make an elderly, portly, agitated and unexercised gentleman very breathless indeed — especially when the station stairs and the seventeen steps up to the sitting room at 221B are added; and that if 221B had been as far away from the station as are the houses in the Nos. 19/35 or 45/67 group, he would have been much more likely to collapse on Holmes' bearskin rug, like Dr Thorneycroft Huxtable in *The Priory School*.

The fact that Holmes banked at a branch of the Capital and Counties Bank in Oxford Street may suggest to some students that 221B was therefore nearer the southern end of Baker Street. But just as there is no evidence that Watson used the nearest post office, so there is none that Holmes patronized the nearest bank. If he had wished to do so, indeed, there was a branch of the National Provincial Bank located at the corner of Dorset Street at that period. But men are notoriously sentimental about their banks, and will often put themselves to inconvenience in order to maintain continuity. So we may take it that the position of the bank throws no light on the position of the house.

Let us now test the claims of Nos. 109/111 and the rest by the main clue of 'turning swiftly down a narrow passage' from Blandford Street as described in *The Empty House.* Narrow passages, parallel with Baker Street, open out of Blandford Street both to north and south. The northward passage is prolonged across Dorset Street and Paddington Street and ends in the cul-de-sac now known as Sherlock Mews. Southward from Blandford Street the passage runs to George Street. It will thus be seen that any house which backs on to these passages anywhere between George Street and Sherlock Mews could be regarded as fulfilling at least one important condition required of 'the empty house' — i.e. that it can be entered in the rear from a narrow passage opening off Blandford Street.

About twenty-five years ago, Dr Gray Chandler Briggs, of St Louis, U.S.A., mapped Baker Street from end to end as a labour of love. Approaching from the rear, he decided that No. 118 Baker Street was the house which best fitted the description of 'the empty house' and that the house opposite, that is, No. 111, must therefore be the original of 221B. As a clincher, he found that No. 118 actually bore the name 'Camden House' as in the story. Of this discovery Vincent Starrett, the doyen of American Sherlockians, wrote: 'No more brilliant identification has been made in our time.'

Mr Ernest Short, for many years secretary of the Authors' Club of which Conan Doyle was a member, also made out a good case for No. 109, particularly by pointing

59

out that Sherlock Mews gives access to the rear of houses which are approximately opposite the block containing Nos. 109/111.

H. W. Bell and T. S. Blakeney both claim that the direction 'down a side passage from Blandford Street' fixes the passage as being either Blandford Mews or Kendal Mews and that 221B must accordingly be one of the houses in the 19/35–45/67 group on the opposite side of Baker Street. I think they both overlook the point that northward from Blandford Street is not merely an isolated alley extending only a few yards but, as I have said, a continuous series of three passages ending in Sherlock Mews beyond Paddington Street. It will be remembered that on the empty house journey Holmes took particular care to avoid being followed. What then more convenient than this sequence of narrow, and doubtless ill-lit, northerly passages along which they could steal not only undetected ('my revolver in my pocket and the thrill of adventure in my heart' as Watson excitingly records) but also in complete conformity with the canon?

Mr Bell and Mr Blakeney also point out that, until 1921, the portion of Baker Street containing Nos. 109 and 111 was known as York Place. Mr Bell stated his objection explicitly: 'In fact, during the entire active career of Sherlock Holmes, and for many years afterwards, the present No. 111 was not in Baker Street at all and was known as No. 30 York Place.' How pettifogging! It is as if one were to argue that Nash's noble curve was not part of Regent Street because it was known at that time as the Quadrant. If Baker Street formerly ended at Crawford Street, the Metropolitan station ought surely to have been named 'York Place Station' or 'Upper Baker Street

Station'. That it has always been called 'Baker Street Station' surely suggests that the whole thoroughfare, from Portman Square to Regent's Park, was always thought of as a single street, just as it is today.

The factors in favour of No. 19, the most southerly house in our groups, were set out by Mr James T. Hyslop in an early issue of *The Baker Street Journal*. His analysis contains a number of strange statements which suggest that his knowledge of London was by no means as exact as that of Mr Holmes. For example, he makes Watson walk across the Park to 221B in '*The Red-headed League*' from *his home near Paddington Station*, ignoring alike the obvious inference that Watson was then living in Kensington, not Paddington, and the equally obvious fact that you would not cross any park on any journey from Paddington Station to any house in Baker Street.

On the assumption that Peterson, the commissionnaire in *The Blue Carbuncle*, must have lived at or near 221B, Mr Hyslop goes on to contend that his presence at the corner of Goodge Street and Tottenham Road must have meant that 221B was at the southern end of Baker Street because 'no man in his senses would try to reach No. 111 by such a route.' But is it not reasonable to suppose that Henry Baker was on his way home from the Alpha Inn when Peterson followed him and that both were therefore walking *northwards* along Tottenham Court Road towards Goodge Street? If Peterson had reached the Goodge Street corner his homeward route would have been along that street to Cavendish Square no matter which end of the street he lived in.

Mr Hyslop is on less shaky ground in his emphasis on the various references to Oxford Street — the fact that they used a boot shop, a tobacco store and so on in that street. Even here, however, I do not feel that anything is proved. Holmes and Watson had many interests in the West End — clubs, concert halls, opera house, picture galleries, and turkish baths, apart from their visits to the Yard and Whitehall — all of which would take them naturally along Oxford Street whichever part of the street they may have inhabited.

A case for No. 27 has been presented by Dr Maurice Campbell in *Sherlock Holmes and Dr Watson: a Medical Digression*. I fear, however, that Dr Campbell's claim that they must have gone *south* from Blandford Street because Watson wrote of turning *down* the passage instead of *up* has no significance. In *The Resident Patient*, for example (and to which I shall return), Watson speaks of being half-way *down* Harley Street when they were in fact proceeding north. Similar descriptions occur in *The Hound* and *The Blue Carbuncle*. All are the exact opposite of Dr Campbell's suggestion.

I have already noted that Gavin Brend expressed a preference for Nos. 59/63, particularly for No. 61 on the amiable discovery that it was formerly occupied by Messrs. Walker and Holtzapffel Ltd. who bear the first two letters of Watson and the first three of Holmes. (In passing, I have always considered myself a 'natural' Sherlockian since the first three letters of my last name — Hol — and the last three letters of my first name — mes — together form the name-of-names!) Moreover, when I told the late Jim Montgomery that my mother's maiden name was Alice Fowler, he immediately proposed me for honorary membership of the Sons of the Copper Beeches of Philadelphia whither the lady in the adventure emigrated after her encounter with the fat and fraudulent Jephro Rucastle. And when I bought Mgr Knox's *Memories of the Future* for the passage in which Opal, Lady Porstock, describes how as an M.P. she sponsored 'the erection of the great statue of Sherlock Holmes in Baker Street', I found to my amazement that the leader of the Opposition at that period was 'the Rt. Hon. James Holroyd'. Mgr Knox's brother, 'Evoe' of *Punch*, suggested that I ought to have threatened him with a libel action!)

Gavin Brend's case for these three numbers was mainly based on walking and cab distances in *The Hound*, but it seems to me that neither of his arguments would preclude 221B from being sited still further north in Baker Street. Indeed, if the reader shares my view that Baker Street was commonly accepted as extending from Portman Square to the corner of Park Road, then the second cabman's estimate of 'half-way down the street' would mean that he pulled up somewhere about the corner of Paddington Street — a point of no value to Mr Brend's 61, but most convenient from which to watch the comings and goings at Nos. 109/111. Incidentally the houses at 59/63 have now disappeared and a new block of offices occupies the site.

So far one has simply eliminated the claim of Abbey House and suggested a tilting of balance (or bias?) in favour of 109/111 against the Blandford Street group. It is time to produce more positive evidence to support the claim of 109/111. I suggest that the clue is to be found — and I first drew attention to its importance in the 1951 summer *Cornhill* — in *The Resident Patient*. It will be recalled that Holmes and Watson were walking home from Brook Street late one October night when Watson recorded that 'We had crossed Oxford Street and were half-way down Harley Street before I could get a word out of my companion.' The significance of this quotation is: *what were they doing half-way down Harley Street?* It was at least 11 pm. Earlier in the evening they had strolled around Fleet Street and the Strand for three hours — a very tiring exercise after a close and rainy day, even if nightfall 'had brought a breeze with it'. When they had first returned to 221B Watson had spoken cosily of 'our sanctum'. One senses a little weariness behind the words — perhaps the old bullet-wound had been aggravated by the hard pavements. On arriving at 221B they had been obliged to listen to the long narrative of Dr Trevelyan, the taper-faced man, had then been whisked off to his 'sombre, flat-faced house' at 403 Brook Street, and were only now on the way back. The canon is quite explicit. They were 'walking for home' — not merely taking a final turn. Even Holmes appears to have been less energetic than usual. At any rate, there is no suggestion of a late supper or even of gasogene and decanter while they con over the problem in dressing-gown and slippers. He says simply — and the phrase is exceptional for him — 'But we may sleep on it now.'

If they were tired, it is reasonable to suppose that they would go home by the most direct route. Now No. 403 Brook Street was clearly a fictitious number; as fictitious, in fact, as No. 221B! But although the number may have been imaginary, there can be little doubt about the position of 403. It must have stood at the extreme eastern end of Brook Street — that is, on the corner of Hanover Square. Why? Because if the house had been sited anywhere west of this point, the obvious way home would

have been Oxford Street–Wigmore Street–Baker Street. To walk home via Harley Street from any other part of Brook Street would have been to walk *away* from Baker Street. From the corner of Hanover Square, however, they could have slipped along Harewood Place, over to Holles Street and across Cavendish Square into Harley Street walking roughly *parallel* with Baker Street all the time.

Thus they could have walked along Harley Street without going out of their way to Baker Street. *But it depends which part of Baker Street.* 'Half-way down Harley Street' is about mid-way between New Cavendish Street and Weymouth Street. Thence into Baker Street one can either take the next turn on the left — Weymouth Street — or further on turn left along Devonshire Street. The important point to note is that while either of these routes is on the direct way for Nos. 109 or 111, they both overshoot the Blandford Street group. Weymouth Street enters Marylebone High Street opposite Paradise Street — 200 yards north of Blandford Street; while Devonshire Street joins the High Street opposite Paddington Street — 300 wasted yards beyond Blandford Street and at least 150 yards north of Gavin Brend's No. 61.

So on the reasonable assumption that the pair were tired and making for home by a route which would not add unnecessary distance, one arrives at the very strong conclusion that 221B was somewhere in the 109/111 block. Having established the approximate site, one has now to choose between the 111 of Dr Chandler Briggs and the 109 of Mr Ernest Short.

I believe that Dr Briggs' choice of 118 as the empty house and therefore of 111 as 221B is open to two fundamental objections. The first of these was noted by H. W.

Bell who pointed out that the rear of 118 cannot be reached direct from the passages from Blandford Street, but only by turning to the right into Paddington Street, left into Chiltern Street, left into Portman Mansions and left again into David Mews. Mr Bell contended — rightly in my view — that this 'long and roundabout route' did not correspond to the requirements quoted in *The Empty House*.

The second factor against Dr Briggs is that from 1885 to 1932 No. 118 was continuously occupied by a high-grade preparatory school known as Camden House School. In the spring of 1894, therefore, its principal ground floor apartment could scarcely have been described as a large empty room with bare creaking planking, windows thick with dust and paper hanging in ribbons from the walls. (The school is now in Gloucester Place.)

The above factors seem to me to rule out Dr Briggs' claim entirely. The original Camden House just will not fit; first because the back is not accessible via the narrow passages from Blandford Street, and also because it could not have been derelict at the time of the adventure.

It is therefore apparent that some other building must have been the 'empty house', just as Mrs Hudson's immortal 221B must have been on some site other than the real 221 Baker Street. The field is thus left clear for Ernest Short who fixes on No. 108, the present Y.W.C.A. hostel, as the original of the empty house and No. 109 opposite as the original 221B. No. 108 is the building which divides Sherlock Mews from David Mews. It has the obvious advantage that the rear can be approached from Sherlock Mews, the last of the chain of three narrow passages leading from Blandford Street. Although Mr Short's No.

108 and No. 109 *en face* are not in exact alignment across Baker Street, I am confident that the angle involved would not have presented any difficulty to Colonel Moran who was described by Holmes as 'the best heavy-game shot our Eastern Empire ever produced'.

My final support for Mr Short's No. 109 is taken from an old map which shows the block between Paddington Street and Portman Mansions as a perfect capital letter 'H' with Sherlock Mews and David Mews (then known respectively as York Mews South and York Mews North) as the spaces and No. 108, the present Y.W.C.A. building, as the crossbar linking the two uprights. H for Holmes, H for John H. Watson, H for Mrs Hudson. . . . With such a signpost there can surely be no doubt that 221B itself must be just across the street. I take my stand on this, for it follows a principle indicated by Holmes himself in *The Boscombe Valley Mystery*: 'You know my method. It is founded upon the observance of trifles.'!

Solutions by Numbers

I have already mentioned the recent American theory of a concealed alternative solution to each story. I wouldn't be surprised if the writer were on the right track; for I had no sooner opted for No. 109 as the true original of 221B than I discovered that the saga was strewn with supporting clues or ciphers which pointed to this number.

The first story I subjected to textual scrutiny of this kind was the improbable *Musgrave Ritual*. It had always seemed to me that its central theme of an ancient jingle leading to the recovery of a lost British crown was a fairy-tale invented by Holmes for the mystification of Dr Watson. Such a theory is perhaps more plausible in that the ritual is one of the few adventures in which the doctor did not take part. Holmes, however, was too clever a craftsman to play a merely pointless joke on Watson, so I was confident that the clues would lead somewhere, if not in the expected direction of lost treasure.

In endeavouring to read the riddle anew, it was clear to me that the most important ingredients in the story were the house (Hurlstone), the family (Musgrave) and the two trees in the ritual (Oak and Elm). As one jotted down the initials of these four words, the meaning became instantly apparent. They spelled out HOME. Whose home? Going back to the story, one found that Sun(S) and Shadow(S) were equally vital to the solution and that the house itself was specifically described as L-shaped. When these letters were added they produced the following arrangement:

S HOLMES

The story, then, was a clue to the identity of the home of S. Holmes as I had suspected. I felt that the game was indeed afoot. Next, there could be no doubt that the most significant figures in the ritual were the pacings — 'by ten and by ten etc.' Recalling the multiplication tables of childhood, I concluded that this expression might signify 'ten *times* ten'. The remaining significant figures — 'the 6th from the 1st' — were also added. Finally, one sensed that the particularizing of the size of the secret chamber (7 by 4) must have some bearing on the mystery; but as it was underground (or as one might say 'below the line'), this figure had to be subtracted, not added. The completed sum thus became:

North	$10 \times 10 = 100$
East	$5 \times 5 = 25$
South	$2 \times 2 = 4$
West	$1 \times 1 = 1$
'The 6th ... the 1st'	$6 + 1 = 7$
	137
Deduct size of underground chamber	$7 \times 4 = 28$
	109

Q.E.D.

This piece of jugglery almost cost me my valued

honorary membership of the Musgrave Ritualists of New York!

My next investigation was *The Red-headed League*. During a discussion of this adventure by members of the Sherlock Holmes Society of London, most members appeared to find difficulty in reconciling some aspect of timing or topography. Thus one member was unable to identify Saxe-Coburg Square; another could not find a way into the Strand which would correspond with John Clay's direction of 'third right, fourth left'; another was baffled by the fact that such a wonderful story on its own doorstep ('Fleet Street was choked with red-headed folk, and Pope's Court looked like a coster's orange barrow') was unaccountably not reported in the Press.

I suggested, heretically, that there was an explanation which would cover all the difficulties. The explanation was simply that the whole thing never happened! Watson, who as we know, was not wanting in a vein of pawky humour at times, was simply pulling the leg of his readers. He brazenly invented the story but neglected to think out the details clearly. (Consider the muddle in dates, for example.) Holmes, again, was too thorough a master of mystery to allow Watson merely to hoax his public. He insisted that the hidden clues in this fine yarn should add up to something, even if not to the thirty thousand Napoleons in the vaults of the City and Suburban Bank.

With these considerations before me, I found that the inner trail led (as, again, I had suspected it would) to the true identity of 221B. If one is looking for the number of a house, I reasoned, one should begin with the numbers of any houses mentioned in the story. First, then, came 7

Pope's Court (later described by Jabez Wilson, the pawnbroker, as No. 4). Also 17 King Edward Street, near St Paul's. These three addresses total 28. Next (though for no apparent reason) we may add the 32 sovereigns received as wages by Wilson and his peculiar hours of duty — 10 to 2. 10 plus 2 equals 12. Add 32 and 12 to 28 and we reach a total of 72.

Finally, one should ask what significance lies in that odd selection of encyclopaedia subjects listed by Wilson: Abbots, Archery, Armour, Architecture, Attica. I had often thought that an elderly Victorian pawnbroker would have been more likely to name some of the items encountered in his day-to-day business such as Accordions, Antimacassars, Antlers, or Aspidistras. Nor would one have been surprised to find him pre-occupied with disease — Adenoids, Adhesions, even Anthrax. Or perhaps with something a trifle *recherché* such as Absinthe or Amber. And then, in a flash, one saw that the subjects were put into his mouth by Watson who had carefully selected words which contained a total of 37 letters. ('My collection of "A's" is a fine one'?) Add 37 to the original 72 and we arrive — would you be surprised to learn? — at a final total of 109.

I also found abundant clues in *The Sign of Four*. Indeed there appeared to be almost as many variations as there were kinds of tobacco ash in Holmes' monograph from the same adventure. Here are examples of how it worked out:

(1) Two of the most significant dates are May 4 (the day Mary Morstan received her pearls) and July 7 (post-mark of Thaddeus Sholto's letter).

May 4	4th of 5th	=	45
July 7	7th of 7th	=	77
			122

add together

Now deduct Mary's 6 pearls and 7 pm, (the meeting time outside the Lyceum Theatre)
6 plus 7   = 13

And the result is   109

(2) It has been suggested that if 1888, not the Jubilee Year of 1887 was the date of the first marriage of Dr Watson, Mary Morstan would have received 7 pearls, not 6. Bearing this in mind, let us take a third significant date, that of Captain Morstan's disappearance on December 3.

December 3   12th month, 3rd day = 123
Now add together the digits of the three
dates 123, 45, 77   = 29
Multiply 29 by the Sign of 4 (why not?) =   116
Deduct the 7 pearls   7

And the result is still   109

(3) Or take that mystic 337 on the *Sign of Four* paper.

Add to it the sum of the digits from example
(2), i.e. 337 + 29   = 366
Now add together the three dates (123, 45, 77) and throw in Holmes' 7 per cent solution of cocaine and the 5th proposition of Euclid (both from the same chapter) and we find a total of   257

Deduct and the answer (of course) is   109

72

(4) Let us now turn an eye on the Agra treasure chest. Surely some of those jewels have more than a passing significance? We will first recall the numbers: 143 diamonds, 97 emeralds, 170 rubies, 40 carbuncles, 210 sapphires, 61 agates and 300 pearls (12 set in a gold coronet).

It will be instantly apparent that if we take the sapphires	= 210
And deduct from them the 61 agates and 40 carbuncles	= 101
The result will be	109
Or add together the 300 pearls and 61 agates	= 361
And subtract 143 diamonds and 97 emeralds	= 240
The result if of course too many	121
But we are told by Jonathan Small that 12 of the pearls set in a gold coronet were missing from the treasure chest. We ought therefore to deduct the 12 pearls	12
Thus giving a final figure of	109

All this is so simple, so obvious, so elementary, that one can only echo Watson's words: 'Holmes, a child has done this horrid thing.'

In case my figuring is regarded as suspect, may I point out that there are other clues which open the door to the identifying of 109 (one-o-nine) as the true original of 221B. These keys are where we should expect to find them — in the opening sentence of each of the three stories quoted:

The Musgrave Ritual: 'An an*O*maly which ofte*N* struck m*E* in

73

the character *Of* my frie*N*d Sherlock Holmes was that, although *IN* his m*E*thods . . . .'

The Red-headed League: 'I had called up*ON* my fri*E*nd, Mr Sherl*O*ck Holmes, o*N*e day *IN* th*E* autumn . . . .'

The Sign of Four: 'Sherlock Holmes took his bottle from the c*Or*N*E*r *Of* the ma*N*telp*I*ece a*N*d his hypod*E*rmic syringe . . . .'

Fanciful Furnishings

On the autumn night of 1951 when the Sherlock Holmes Festival Year Exhibition was closing down a few of us gathered disconsolately around Michael Weight's wonderful reconstruction of the 221B sitting room in Abbey House. There in the mellow glow of the lamps was the familiar scene — the armchairs by the fire, the bearskin rug for Dr Thorneycroft Huxtable to collapse on; violin, riding crop, Persian slipper with tobacco, pipes, handcuffs, lens, even a knuckleduster in the butter-dish: all were there, every piece falling into its appointed place in the canon — and in the affections.

The exhibition was to be dismantled before starting on a world tour. We should probably never see it again. And as the lights were being turned out one by one I found myself quoting from *His Last Bow*: 'Stand with me here upon the terrace, for it may be the last quiet talk that we shall ever have.'

But the dream came to life again at the end of 1957 when Whitbreads, with a fine imaginative gesture, renamed a pub in Northumberland Street, Charing Cross, the 'Sherlock Holmes', displayed a fascinating selection of material from the exhibition round the walls and — 'Holmes, this is wonderful,' I cried — divided the grillroom by a broad plate-glass window through which one

75

could gaze anew at the immortal sitting room, just as it was in the exhibition, just as it is for ever enshrined in the stories.

The apartment is naturally on the first floor. (I am ashamed to say that, like Watson, I cannot recall how many steps lead up to it.) Although within 150 yards of the 'ever-changing kaleidoscope' of the Strand, it is so quiet that one can hear the clock ticking out the minutes of 1895. One feels that Holmes and Watson, whose deerstalker and professional silk hat hang behind the door, have doubtless stepped out to the Turkish baths round the corner or gone to visit Sir Henry Baskerville in the Northumberland Hotel a few yards away.

The 'Sherlock Holmes' gives a true touch of 'character' to a familiar corner of London. My friend Louis Wulff of the *Evening News* had an amusing experience there soon after it opened. He had arranged to meet a friend, but was delayed and so telephoned the manager to ask him to pass on the message. Although the friend was visiting the S.H. for the first time the manager came across to him immediately and said, 'I believe you are Mr Dunsford. I have a message for you from Mr Louis Wulff'. The friend reflected on this over his drink. When Louis arrived a little later his friend told him that he had received the message but wondered how the manager had identified him so readily. 'You know my methods, Watson,' quoted Louis, 'but let's ask him.' 'Easy,' said the manager. 'I just looked round the bar and as there was only one person there I didn't recognize I knew he must be Mr Dunsford.' Elem — anyway it was good to have this early assurance that the place was being conducted on well-established principles!

It is perhaps ungracious to look too deeply into the

sources of one's delight but I am ready to admit that I have
a special private interest in the reconstruction of the Baker
Street sitting room. It is that if I ever have the spare
accommodation (and the reluctant consent of my wife) I
intend to assemble a similar apartment in my own home.
What could be more agreeable than to retreat at will into
so delectable a past? The closest approach I have at the
moment is a large water-colour drawing of the interior of
the Holborn Restaurant as in Watson's day. It brightens
my office wall and on many of those days when the world
is too much with us I have stepped into the picture and
helped myself to a glass of wine — pre-phylloxera, of
course — from one of those gleaming decanters.

In paissng, I have always supposed that Dr Watson
lunched young Stamford at the Holborn not merely because it was on the way to Bart's Hospital where he was to
meet Holmes for the first time but because he knew a thing
or two about good living. I had confirmation of this in an
advertisement of a booklet for the year 1880. The restaurant
then apparently combined 'the attractions of the Chief
Parisien Establishments with the quiet and order essential
to English customs.' From 5.30 to 8.30 each day they put
on a *table d'hôte* dinner 'at separate tables in the Grand
Salon, the Prince's Salon and the Duke's Salon'. It included two soups, two kinds of fish, two entrees, joints,
sweets, cheese (in variety), salad, etc., with ices and des-
sert. The dinner was accompanied by 'a Selection of high-
class Instrumental Music'. The price was 3s. 6d. All this
and Holborn too!

To return to my dream of a sanctum in the style of 221B,
I have for a long time played an inexhaustible private
game of choosing the appropriate pieces of furniture from

junk and antique shops in various parts of London. I could take you tomorrow to a window where you would see two armchairs with carved wooden frames, castors and up-holstery of buttoned leather. They are going very cheaply. For all one knows, they may be *the* chairs. I have also peered long and lovingly at sofas with scroll ends and shiny horse-hair bolsters. I know that particular type well; as a boy I often sat on one and the sharp protruding fibres prickled the backs of my legs. (Why were the Victorians so unrecking of the small sweet comforts? Need life always have been quite so earnest, quite so real?)

Sometimes I try to interest her ladyship in these imaginary purchases. I point out one of those mobile paper-racks known as Canterburys — a ravishing piece of old English walnut with a shallow drawer at its base. The compartments are divided by elegant spindles and lattices. 'See how convenient,' I say, 'You would be able to keep all your women's magazines there as well as the *Globe, Star, Pall Mall, St. James's Gazette, Evening News, Standard, Echo*, and any others that occur to you.' Her laconic reply is: 'Dust-traps.'

Or I point out the bargain prices at which one could snap up such unconsidered trifles as large framed repro-ductions of 'The Monarch of the Glen' or 'When did you last see your Father?', a globe of stuffed birds or waxed fruit, an elephant's foot umbrella-stand of the kind Wat-son may well have brought back from the East, or a brass letter balance with only three small weights missing. Of such ampler treasures of the might-have-been, I have succeeded in bringing home only one — a stirring depic-tion of the stand made by the last eleven at Maiwand. I cannot doubt that it would have evoked the clenched fist, the hand stealing towards the old wound, and indeed the whole emotional chain-reaction of the good doctor in his brown study. And I have to record with regret that at the moment it lives with its face to the wall in a dark corner of the flat.

Pending the day when I shall have my own 221B, I have nevertheless been able to give my collecting mania an airing of sorts by assembling a number of miniature 'association' items on top of the bookshelves which hold my Sherlockian volumes. There at various times may be seen a diminutive tantalus, midget handcuffs, a thumbling Napoleon, a small hansom-cab, a six-inch model lamp-post (the appropriate quotation here is not the dog in the night-time), a silver place-holder in the shape of a striking cobra, a pocket edition of the complete peerage for 1895. You may be sure that the shelf also holds a pocket flask and a cigar case, a Persian slipper and an assortment of pipes. Perhaps a trifle *recherché* are the opium-pipe from the Bar of Gold, the silver medal of the Afghan War, the sovereign-purse with its spring lid, the corded bell-pull with its opulent rosette, the tiny alabaster bust of a certain gracious lady. Among them is a magnifying glass with a beautifully scrolled silver handle. Above the rows of books it also seemed appropriate that there should be portraits of General Gordon and Henry Ward Beecher (unframed).

I recommend this Baker Street by-way to fellow Sherlockians. With patience they may acquire the gold snuff-box with the massive amethyst in the lid presented by the King of Bohemia; the match-box in which Isadora Persano ('the wellknown journalist and duellist') lodged the worm unknown to science, the square Chinese coin which hung from Jabez Wilson's watch-chain, the Ming saucer, the blue carbuncle, the Mazarin stone — perhaps even the Black Pearl of the Borgias. On reflection the latter would of course be too precious for open display. One would have to keep it in the safe along with the papers of the celebrated forgery case.

6 'The ever-changing kaleidoscope of life . . . through Fleet
Street and the Strand' as Holmes and Watson saw it at the
period of *The Resident Patient* or *The Red-headed League*

7 Pall Mall looking east with a hansom turning into Lower Regent Street. Mycroft Holmes, brother of Sherlock, had his rooms and club in Pall Mall. The meeting of the brothers at the Diogenes on a fine summer evening was

'Our Sanctum'

'The best detective stories ever written,' said the late Christopher Morley, 'usually begin with a scene of domestic interior: Holmes and Watson on either side of the Baker Street hearth.' That indeed is the setting in which the world knows them best. Evening has set in and the wild weather without gives greater emphasis to the snugness within. The heavy curtains have been drawn and the firelight flickers cosily on the polished wood of the side-board or strikes an answering gleam from the bottles and retorts on the chemical table in the corner. Holmes is deep in one of his esoteric studies — the polyphonic motets of Lassus or some medieval palimpsest — while Watson runs an eye over some professional journal or, more likely we feel, revels in one of his yellow-backs. The scene is set for a cab to drive up to the door and for a new adventure to begin.

Yet as the curtain rises on the most familiar interior in the world, we may suddenly realise that there is much we have never known regarding its precise details. Chris Morley was right, as always, in showing the partners at ease by their own fireside. But in fact no-one has ever been quite certain which sat on the right and which on the left, nor indeed just where the fireplace stood.

What, moreover of the sitting-room itself? When we ask

the most elementary question as to whether it was large or small, doubt enters with us at the door. Watson first describes it in *A Study in Scarlet* as 'a single large airy sitting-room, cheerfully furnished'. Yet in the adventure of *The Resident Patient* he speaks of being 'weary of our little sitting-room' and when Sir James Damery comes to see them on behalf of the illustrious client he records that 'the big masterful aristocrat dominated the little room'.

To judge from the substantial quantity of furniture mentioned at various times one would suppose the room to have been reasonably large. As a minimum it had to accommodate two arm chairs, basket chair, wooden chair, dining table and chairs, sofa, settee, table for chemicals, two desks, two book-cases, coal scuttle, safe, shelves for reference material. Much research has been focussed on the subject. Dr Jay Finley Christ has catalogued 150 items of furniture. But his entertaining theory is that all this gear was not on hand simultaneously but — like so many stage properties — was wheeled in and out by Mrs Hudson as required by the drama of the moment.

Careful plans dealing with the disposition of the furniture are published in *The Baker Street Journal* from time to time. One notes that Dr Julian Wolff and Mr R. Spearman Myers both put Holmes on the left side of the fireplace, while Mr Ernest Short sited his armchair on the right-hand side. Nor can the problem be solved by reference to the numerous illustrators, for they show the pair sitting now one side, now the other. Sidney Paget customarily put Holmes on the right-hand side. (Until recently the actual arm-chair in which he so often reclined was in the possession of the Paget family and the original cane chair which first appeared in *The Greek Interpreter* now forms part of the sitting-room reconstruction in the upper room at the 'Sherlock Holmes'.)

The door into the sitting-room at 221B is another of the baffling pieces in the jig-saw. Mr Myers puts it in the wall facing the windows, that is, on the west side of the room, but Dr Wolff and Mr Short allocate it to the north wall.

But if No. 109 is accepted as the true original of 221B, then the door to the sitting-room would have to be on the south wall since the street door and stairway are on that side of the building. The same goes for No. 111. This reveals a curious error on Mr Short's calculations; for he cannot opt for No. 109 and at the same time draw the street door on the north or right-hand-side of the house when it is in fact on the south or left-hand side. (It has been suggested that the field is still open for a completely new investigation of the site of 221B if some diligent researcher is able to locate the solitary plane tree which Watson could see from his bedroom at the back of the house.)

There is also an engaging waywardness in the way the door opens, now left, now right. Perhaps it achieves its greatest individuality in *A Case of Identity* in which it consecutively opens inwards, hinged left; inwards, hinged right; outwards, hinged right! I think the door was entitled to this display of temperament, for we have been asked to believe that the girl in the story did not recognize her rascally step-father when he took her to the Gas Fitters' Ball disguised as her lover. It seems to me as improbable a situation as when Mrs St Clair failed to identify her husband in the accents of *The Man With the Twisted Lip*. A further peculiar feature about the door in *A Case of Identity* is that in the Paget illustration in which said step-father glances around like a rat in a trap, the knob and keyhole are shown some distance down the lower panel. The door-handle is thus less than three feet from the ground. There is also a finger-panel *below* it. This is about the height of a nursery door-handle. Could the previous occupants of the rooms have been a family with young children?

It is instructive to note that George Hutchinson, Paget's contemporary, also had door trouble. For the entry of the urchin troop of 'irregulars' in *A Study in Scarlet* it opens inwards, hinged on the left, yet when Holmes and Co. are examining the mongrel dog later in the story the door-knob is on the left which means that the door must have been hinged on the right.

The fireplace also presents problems. If we accept Nos. 109/11, whose doors were on the south side, plus the general agreement that the windows were on the east wall, then it would be reasonable to place the fireplace either on the north or west wall. Hutchinson's 'stag-hounds' illustration shows it to be on the north wall, but other artists have depicted it on the south, west, and even east between the tall windows looking down into Baker Street.

It would of course have been intolerably dull if Watson had inventoried every item in the apartment. Instead, good artist as he was, he was content to mention them as they were spotlighted by events — the bearskin rug only when Dr Huxtable falls athwart it, the wooden chair only when it serves as a peg for the battered bowler of Mr Henry Baker. Any illustrator worthy of his steel would clearly feel at liberty to sketch in any reasonable details even though they were not specifically named in the saga. There is a special pleasure in entering the sanctum with this thought in mind. For example, when Holmes reappeared in the *Strand* after an interval of eight years, the first things one noticed were the decorative plates above the lintel of the door. A new hobby? In the same illustration a wooden carving chair is introduced for the first time, while in a later chapter of the *Hound* we are shown a small octagonal Indian coffee-table, obviously a Watsonian touch to remind him of old campaigning days.

Hutchinson's *A Study in Scarlet* presents us with five non-canonical pictures, all, alas, undecipherable save the last where in a wild and stormy landscape one is just able to pick out a microscopic horseman galloping into the livid west. A reminiscence of the Vernets, perhaps? James Greig's realization of the room, in the same story, has a touch of elegance. Holmes and Watson both wear winged collars, frock coats and light trousers. Two alabaster lamps are reflected in the wide mirror above the mantelshelf; a statuette poses a dainty limb in the angle of the walls. There is a hint of a palm tree. The only lapse is that although there are a couple of 'easies' in the drawing, Watson is offering the 'old lady' a strictly utilitarian rush-bottomed kitchen chair.

Speculation has arisen as to whether there were any other lodgers at Mrs Hudson's boarding house at 221B. Vincent Starrett thinks not. 'Holmes would surely have complained of them (or they of him),' he says, 'and we should have had some record of them in Watson's pages.' Yet I have sometimes wondered whether there is not a hint of another tenant in *The Resident Patient*. Holmes and Watson return after their three-hour stroll around Fleet Street to find a doctor's brougham outside the door. Holmes' immediate 'Come to consult us, I fancy,' is confirmed by Watson's slower-footed reasoning: 'The light in our window above showed that this late visit was indeed intended for us.' Both these remarks suggest that the visit might have been meant for someone else. But surely not for Mrs Hudson or Billy the page? They would be unlikely to command a call from a fashionable Brook Street doctor late at night. Moreover, at the period of the story, two other doctors were living in Baker Street, not to mention Dr Watson himself. So who was the other tenant at 221B? Remembering the indoor revolver practice, the wailing violin in the small hours, the setting alight of the rooms, the criminals throwing themselves through the window, and so on, one ought perhaps to describe him as the Patient Resident.

But this is heresy. The building remains inviolate for all time as the address of Holmes and Watson alone. So there we may leave them in the place that fits them like a glove — the cosy sitting-room with the cheerful fire. ('Our sanctum' Watson called it in the story already quoted and one warms to the phrase.) The wind is sobbing like a child in the chimney and the distances of Baker Street are glazed with rain. A long evening stretches ahead, timeless as eternity. For us, as for Vincent Starrett, that is how the room remains in memory: 'Little vignettes of perfect happiness, wreathed in tobacco smoke and London fog.'

The Shaggiest Dog

It was in 1901–2 that the Hound of the Baskervilles first leapt across the pages of the old *Strand Magazine* and stirred the world with the faint promise that Holmes might indeed be less dead than dormant. Although the author had ruthlessly killed off his detective at the Reichenbach Falls some years previously, there can be no doubt that he enjoyed writing this earlier episode of a ghost-hound which in the end was seen to be a creature of flesh and blood. 'A real creeper' was how he described the adventure in a letter to his mother. To many who regard it as his finest story, this seems no more than due praise.

The amazing and seemingly imperishable appeal of the *Hound* is apparent alike in translation and illustration. One senses its sinister and baleful aura glimmering through the titles of Irish, Norwegian and Polish editions: CU NA MBASKERVILLE, HUNDEN FRA BASKERVILLE, PIES BASKERVILLE' OW. The climax of the story, when the great hound emerges from the mist on the track of the unsuspecting baronet, is a natural which has attracted many artists ranging from the flaming apparition by H. M. Brock to the slavering horror depicted by Frederic Dorr Steele, the American.

Sidney Paget, whose original illustrations in the *Strand Magazine* contained some of his best work, nevertheless achieved several odd slips. In the drawings of the legendary hound, for instance, the costume of the horsemen belongs to the eighteenth century instead of to the seventeenth as required by the text. On the moor Holmes is given a soft felt hat though the description demands a cloth cap. And Lestrade, who wears a cap as he hides behind the rocks, sports a bowler a couple of pictures later when he starts — a bad third — in pursuit of the huge beast.

In passing, my friend Bill McGowran, of the *London Evening News*, has a theory that Lestrade was a tippler and that this explains the fact that while we first meet him as an inspector, he is still the same rank twenty years later. As evidence of inebriety Bill cites Lestrade's reply when Holmes asks if he is armed: 'As long as I have my trousers, I have a hip-pocket, and as long as I have my hip-pocket I have something in it.' He maintains that this is an equivocation because when the Hound appears it is the shots of Holmes and Watson which ring out together, the little detective having flung himself face downwards on the ground with a yell of terror. The pay-off as to what he in fact kept in his hip-pocket occurs a few lines later: 'Lestrade thrust his brandy-flask between the baronet's teeth . . .'! When the Sherlock Holmes Exhibition was held in London during Festival Year, numerous items testified to the continuing interest in the *Hound*. Among these were an excellent copy of the 'faded MS' which recounted the old legend; a plaster paw cast, supplied by Scotland Yard; and stills from films featuring Basil Rathbone and Eille Norwood. What the Exhibition omitted to record was that in 1945 an American found a copy of a film 'Der Hund von Baskerville' in Hitler's private library at Berchtesgaden.

The locale of the story is traditionally Dartmoor and indeed there are several specific references to Princetown and the West Country. Dr Maurice Campbell has nevertheless edged a quiet doubt into the picture by noting that at Kington in Herefordshire, there is a gloomy-looking house with a sombre double avenue, a legend of the Black Dog of Hergest, and — as a clinching touch — a local pub called the Baskerville Arms. Controversy may well march resoundingly down that sombre double avenue for years to come.

Incidentally I should be grateful if any Lestrade among my readers could tell me the reason for Conan Doyle's variation in the dedications of the English and American editions of the *Hound*. Both begin 'My dear Robinson' but continue as follows:

English: 'It was to your account of a West-country legend that this tale owes its inception. For this and for your help in the details all thanks.'

American: 'It was your account of a West country legend which first suggested the idea of this little tale to my mind. For this, and for the help which you gave me in its evolution, all thanks.'

Any re-reading of the *Hound* cannot fail to capture anew those magnificent strokes which bespeak the supreme story-teller — the clink of a stone as Watson waits in the lonely hut on the moor; the death of the convict in the dusk (a scene 'glimpsed by match-spurts and moonlight' as John Dickson Carr notes in his fine biography of Conan Doyle); and the unforgettably thrilling whisper of Dr Mortimer: 'Mr Holmes, they were the footprints of a gigantic hound!'

89

There is also a fair sprinkling of what Christopher Morley has called 'pure Victorian corn' and the reader will re-discover with affection such gems as the baronet's 'By thunder' which is straight from Long John Silver or Holmes' 'This time we have a foreman who is worthy of our steel' which somehow echoes all the author's pre-occupation with medieval chivalry and remains my favourite quotation. (I have a Danish school reader in which the line is flattened into 'This time we fight a dangerous man' — not at all the same thing.)

'Evoe' once advanced the enchanting theory that the story was originally written in verse as a libretto. This was among the examples he quoted in support:

> I stooped and pressed my pistol
> To the dreadful shimmering head,
> But it was useless to press the trigger,
> The giant hound was dead.

'There are moments', he wrote, 'when one seems to hear the choir of a thousand voices.'

A good deal of dogginess is scattered about the Holmes stories: 'The old hound is the best' and so on. It will also be recalled that one of the most famous passages in the saga deals with 'The curious incident of the dog in the night-time':

> 'But the dog did nothing in the night-time'
> 'That was the curious incident.'

In other places Watson not infrequently likens Holmes to a dog on the trail. Readers who were reared on the Sacred Writings will scarcely need to be reminded that

The Shaggiest Dog

George Hutchinson's frontispiece to *A Study in Scarlet* which shows Jefferson Hope hurling himself backwards through the sitting-room window at 221B, is captioned 'Lestrade and Holmes sprang upon him like so many stag-hounds'.

I have often wondered whether the gaunt mastiff of *The Copper Beeches* might not be regarded as the prototype for the Hound of the Baskervilles. Both at least are described as being as big as large calves; both go for the throat of their man; both are despatched by revolver shots. (These, incidentally, are two of the rare sounds of actual gunfire in the stories, despite a considerable flourishing of small arms by Holmes and Watson alike).

There the resemblance ends, however. For while the guardian of *The Copper Beeches* is conventionally called Carlo, Conan Doyle saw at once that the blood-chilling creature which infested the great Grimpen mire must be nameless. It is the more remarkable that this perceptiveness should have failed him at the close of the story. In one sense it makes the monster to be the shaggiest dog of them all. At any rate, I shall never forget the dismay of realizing in after years that the spectral Hound, which haunted my boyhood, had originally been 'bought in London from Ross and Mangles, the dealers in Fulham Road'!

Sherlock Holmes in Regent Street

One of Sidney Paget's most evocative drawings is that from the *Hound* which shows Holmes and Watson encountering the black-bearded man in the hansom-cab in Regent Street. With its leisurely horse traffic, awnings over the shop windows and peaked capped messenger (commissionaire?) in the middle distance, it is a nostalgic period piece. The partners, it will be remembered, were following Sir Henry Baskerville and Dr Mortimer whom they had just interviewed at 221B. As the visitors went downstairs Holmes had changed in an instant 'from the languid dreamer to the man of action' with the immortal words, 'Your hat and boots, Watson, quick! Not a moment to lose'. They had then followed the baronet and his companion along Baker Street and Oxford Street to the point in Regent Street where Holmes sees the hansom and cries, 'There's our man, Watson!'

But although Sidney Paget perfectly realized this exciting moment of the adventure, many readers are probably unaware that the illustration has always been printed the wrong way round in the English editions. Yet an elementary application of Holmes' own methods leaves little doubt that he and Watson ought to be looking at the passenger in the hansom-cab over their right shoulder, not their left. In the first place, Watson is depicted walking with his stick in his left hand, while his morning-coat is buttoned right-over-left instead of left-over-right. One could not judge by the stick alone, for although Paget's drawings of Watson with his pistol in *The Speckled Band* and *The Copper Beeches*, for instance, indicate the doctor's right-handedness, he is also shown in *The Red-headed League* and again on one of his Dartmoor walks and elsewhere with a stick in his left hand. Could it be that he was ambidexterous?

As additional proof that the illustration is printed in reverse, it will be noted that the retreating bus travels close to the *right-hand* kerb and that its stairs descend to the *off* side — an impossible position. Most significant of all is the fact that although Paget usually signed his work in a bold hand, the signature was partially erased when the illustration was first printed in the *Strand* in September 1901. Yet if we whip out our pocket lens we shall see that the faint signature is just decipherable, as it is also on the reproduction in the first English book edition in 1902, and that in both cases it appears back to front. ('I found what I expected to find,' as Holmes cryptically remarked on another occasion!) The legend on the side of the advancing horse bus also appears in looking-glass fashion, but emerges under scrutiny as an advertisement for the 'Hippodrome'.

I think the explanation of this reversed printing in the *Strand* is that as the picture was to appear on a left-hand page of the magazine, the editor had the block made in this way so that Holmes and Watson would face *inwards* — a common journalistic convention in handling illustrations. But although the first English book edition in 1902 continued the inaccuracy, the first American edition of the same year printed the illustration the correct way round. The late Christopher Morley held the odd opinion that this was done to show traffic moving on the *right*-hand side of the street — presumably to conform to American requirements. This would have implied that Paget, who was London born, had actually drawn the traffic on the wrong side of the street in his native heath. One has only to glance at the correct version, however, to see that this was not the case. The retreating bus is properly on the left-hand side of the roadway and has its staircase correctly descending to the left or near side; while the advancing bus is in the middle of the road to avoid the slower traffic nearer the kerb.

Incidentally, the reproduction in the American editions is probably a touched-up version since Holmes has been given a striped collar and shirt-front — a liberty which appears to verge on the impious as well as the improbable. As a further parenthesis, there is matter for speculation about Watson's reactions to whiling away the rest of the morning in 'one of the Bond Street picture galleries'. All very well for Holmes, who was descended from Vernet, the French artist. But Watson had little in common with the long-haired boys, although later at Baskerville Hall he advanced the opinion that Holmes 'had the crudest ideas on painting'. His own picture gallery, we recall, was limited to portraits of General Gordon and Henry Ward Beecher; and while in literature it is true that he once spent an afternoon with Murger's *Vie de Boheme*, his more customary solace was one of Clark Russell's fine sea stories or a current medical book. Could it be that honest Watson put up with these esoteric excursions of Holmes as part of his devoted hero worship? From what we know of Watson's tastes, it seems similarly unlikely that he found any acute pleasure in accompanying Holmes (see *The Red-headed League*) 'to violin land, where all is sweetness, and delicacy, and harmony.' One can imagine his embarrassment on this occasion when Holmes sat in the stalls 'gently waving his long thin fingers in time to the music'. Holmes was really rather selfish in such matters since he must have realized Watson's limitations. In *Sherlock Holmes and Music* Guy Warrack suggests that when they went to hear the de Reskes in Meyerbeer's 'Les Huguenots' (as recorded at the close of the *Hound*) Watson probably fell asleep as a result of their little dinner at Marcini's and that in consequence Holmes did not invite him to the opera again for about ten years.

One curious point about the reversed illustration nevertheless remains. Although we know that the appearances in the *Strand Magazine* and the English book editions were incorrect, the background, with Regent Street curving away to the right, fits the textual fact that Holmes and Watson were walking south from Oxford Street. One would suppose them to have been somewhere on the west side opposite the Cafe Royal. In the correct version the background of course curves to the left, but this does not accord with the canon. One would have to stand in Lower Regent Street to look north and see the background curving to the left. Holmes and Watson in this version would in fact be walking southwards on the east side of Lower Regent Street. As I have earlier argued that Baker Street and Upper Baker Street are both parts of the same thoroughfare, I naturally accept any suggestion that 'walking down Regent Street' could include walking down Lower Regent Street. I will go further and concede that as

Regent Street may be taken to extend from Oxford Circus to the corner of Pall Mall, the hansom could conceivably have been south of Piccadilly Circus at the moment the driver was ordered to whip up his cab — a point which he described precisely as 'when we got three-quarters down Regent Street'. What does not fit, however, is that while the background goes off correctly to the left, it appears as a concave curve; whereas, being in reality the County Fire Office corner, it ought to be straight or slightly convex.

These discrepancies are baffling for the whole scene, whichever way round, has a striking air of actuality, of having been drawn from life. Sidney Paget would doubtless have dismissed such inconsistencies as permissible liberties of the artist; and we may suppose that Conan Doyle would have indulgently replied that 'art in the blood etc.'.

One nevertheless wonders whether Paget may not have had to work too hurriedly on occasion. This would be an explanation of his imperfect reading of the text and his not infrequent minor errors. In the illustration under discussion, for instance, the black-bearded passenger is staring directly at Holmes and Watson and not through the side window of the cab as required by the canon. Again, by the time the pair arrive at the Northumberland Hotel, Holmes (looking rather like a rural dean) is in possession of Watson's walking-stick, while Watson has somehow contrived to shed his white waistcoat for a black one and now wears a handkerchief in his breast pocket. Or consider the door of the sitting room at 221B whose vagaries I have already referred to in an earlier chapter.

Yet, despite infelicities of this kind, Paget was undoubtedly the best known of all illustrators of the chronicle.

And although he may have been an artist of many loyalties — one finds his drawings in such typical early *Strand* titles as Grant Allen's *The Great Ruby Robbery* and Mrs Baumer Williams' *A Palpitating Interview* in the intervals of doing his famous work on the Holmes stories — it must not be forgotten that he was intimately associated with Conan Doyle and that his delineations therefore carry the mark of authority. Perhaps, indeed, his lapses were sometimes deliberate. It is a happy thought that both author and illustrator may have had many a quiet joke over the odd trip-wires they left lying around for the officious.

One of the delights of Sherlockian research is that there is always a little left over for the other fellow. ('I thought I had squeezed all the juice out of it but I see there was a little over,' was Inspector Baynes' word for it.) I therefore suggest that the *aficionado* who can decipher, and thereby identify, the names over the shops in Sidney Paget's Regent Street drawing will settle the matter of precisely where and which side of the street beyond all conjecture. To begin with, one of them carries an emblem which suggests that it was under Royal patronage. It is a clue which would have appealed to Holmes himself; for his successful intervention in many affairs of State must frequently have brought him under Royal notice. The patriotic V.R.s traced in pistol bullets attested his loyalty; and although he refused a knighthood he was wearing an emerald tiepin after a visit to Windsor.

Pistol Packing Partners

I have suggested that although Holmes and Watson make great play with their revolvers throughout the saga, they hardly ever use them. Indeed, their total bag in a partnership extending over so many years appears to have been one hound each (Holmes, Baskervilles; Watson, Copper Beeches) and one 'unhallowed dwarf' shared (*The Sign of Four*). This is little enough in a chronicle which embraces such diverse aids to thuggery as harpoon, battle-axe, blowpipe, nail-studded club, life preserver, noiseless airgun, sawn-off shotgun, wooden leg, long-bladed knife and heavy oaken cudgel.

Holmes' favourite weapon, as we know, was a loaded riding-crop. Some American critics claim that this was because he was an indifferent shot. They believe that he whipped out his pistol and clapped it to a man's head because that was the only position in which he could be sure of hitting his target. They instance the episode of *The Three Garridebs* when Holmes clobbers Killer Evans with the butt of his revolver rather than risk an uncertain shot when Watson is wounded. They hint that Watson tried to cover this deficiency in the Master by recording that 'our shots rang out together and it was clear that one of us had hit him'.

In the light of these speculations one is inclined to see a

new significance in familiar episodes. For example, I have often wondered why in the early morning chase with Toby in *The Sign of Four* Holmes should first have carried an empty revolver and then have loaded it in only two chambers. Could it be that he first relied on bluff and responded with a hint of frugality only when action might be necessary — as if two cartridges were sufficient for a pistoleer of his calibre to waste? Was Moriarty in the secret? When he unexpectedly appeared in the sitting room of 221B he told Holmes that it was a dangerous habit to finger loaded firearms in the pocket of one's dressing gown. Was there a hint of mockery in the admonition? Was this why the Napoleon of crime felt that such derisory tricks as whizzing a two-horse van round a corner and pushing bricks off a roof were suitable methods of attacking Holmes? And Colonel Moran, Moriarty's henchman and 'torpedo' as he would have been described in gangster terms. Surely that rather elementary business of rolling rocks down the Gemmi and the Reichenbach cliff held a note of the most ultimate irony?

Against these strictures, we must recall that when Holmes inserted only two cartridges he may have been acting with characteristic arrogance and that this could have been the gesture of an expert, not an amateur. We must also include Watson's record that one of the Master's annoying indoor pastimes was to sit with a hair-trigger revolver and 100 Boxer cartridges and trace patriotic V.R.s on the walls of the sitting-room at 221B. But here again American research comes cranking in with the information that had the Master indeed used such ammunition in such quantity he would have brought down half the walls of the apartment. Another nice piece of ballistics from the same quarter has demonstrated that a shot fired from across the street at ground level could not possibly have passed through the head of the wax bust of Holmes on the first floor and then buried itself in the wall behind (*The Empty House*).

I believe that one sound reason which prevented our pistol packing partners from using their revolvers — if only to fire warning shots — was that on many occasions they were on dubious or questionable ground. Sir George Burnwell was a typical stage villain as can be seen from his moustache and frogged smoking-jacket in Paget's drawing for *The Beryl Coronet*, but it is clear that Holmes would never have dared use his pistol in the life-preserver episode. Holmes and Watson are avowedly trespassing in Appledore Towers, Hampstead, when they see the veiled visitor empty her tiny revolver at 'the worst man in London'. ('Take that, you hound, and that! — and that! — and that! — and that!') But what legal standing had they in the manor house at Stoke Moran? Holmes lashed at the speckled band with his cane because if he had tried to shoot it Dr Roylott would probably have burst into the bedroom and slung both of them off the premises. (I always re-read with particular pleasure that bit where Holmes, finding the saucer of milk in the doctor's study, asks if they keep a cat. No; no cat, says Miss Enid, the bright girl: but we have a cheetah and a baboon!)

Even more irregular is the scene in pursuit of the Aurora (*The Sign of Four*) where Holmes and Watson produce the firearms and do the shooting although they are aboard a police launch with two inspectors in attendance. Incidentally no fewer than fourteen police officers appear in the saga; but with the exception of Lestrade — and he never finally discloses what he carries in his hip-pocket — I do not recollect that any of them were armed.

As an old campaigner Watson can usually be relied upon to have a revolver somewhere handy; that is, if he feels that a heavy stick is inadequate. In *The Speckled Band* Holmes refers to Watson's revolver as an Eley's No. 2. Some years ago I felt we were on the edge of promising new research when a Sherlockian student told me he had reason to suppose that an Eley's No. 2 was a small yacht cannon! One imagined the chaffing from the Master as Watson positioned his artillery: 'You and your old yacht cannon!' In one case the boot appears to have been on the other foot, when Holmes is seen lugging an enormous piece of small-arms from his pocket with both hands in an illustration to *Lady Frances Carfax*.

Some light on the variety and prices of firearms in 221B days is given in the catalogue of an 'International Sportsman's Exhibition', held at Kensington in 1887, which recently came into my possession. In that period it was possible to buy a 6-shot bright barrel, walnut stock, 320 cal. for 4s 6d or ditto blued barrel 5s 0d. Also advertised was a 'Bull-dog, 6-shot, C.F., D.A., Nickelled, Black Chequered Stock, Round Barrel, 320 cal' — obviously the weapon for Lestrade — for 10s 6d. I also noticed a promising implement called 'the cyclists' road clearer' but this on nearer inspection proved to be a whistle, not a weapon. Also included in the exhibition was the curious black-Peter-like combination of 'harpoon guns and revolvers', 'a new kind of Pocket Revolver for protection, etc.' and, somewhat *recherché*, this one, 'The "Dumonthier" Walking Stick Gun, exactly similar to an ordinary walking stick, weighing but 1 lb.' One feels that Colonel

Moran, as well as Holmes and Watson, would have been at home among such treasures.

I did not, however, find any reference in the catalogue to yacht cannon and Watson must therefore be left to patrol the pages of the saga with nothing more picturesque than his old Service revolver in his pocket. What better final glimpse of his character than when he declines to use it against the convicted murderer at large on Dartmoor? 'A lucky long shot of my revolver might have crippled him, but I had brought it only to defend myself if attacked, and not to shoot an unarmed man who was running away.'

Good old Watson!

Dr Watson and Mr Wilde

The standing warning against mixing Sherlockian fact and fiction was the late Dorothy Sayers' hazard that the master was a Cambridge man because she had found that a T. S. Holmes was at Sidney Sussex in the appropriate years. This painstaking piece of research was shot down drily but decisively by Sir Sidney Roberts who pointed out, almost as an aside, that this Holmes in fact became the Chancellor of Wells Cathedral.

Miss Sayers might nevertheless have returned the fire, for one of Sir Sidney's own speculations was that Dr Watson's full names were John Henry, having been named after Newman by his pious mother. Dare one suggest that Sir Sidney was confusing his cardinals and should have stuck to Tosca?

For my part, I take Dr John Byrom's line:

> But which pretender is and which is king;
> God bless us all, that's quite another thing.

Just as I believe that the Sherlockian umbrella is big enough to accommodate those *aficionados* who believe that Dr Watson wrote the stories as well as those who give the credit to his friend, Sir Arthur Conan Doyle.

This laboured defence has been contrived merely as a

preface to the coincidence that the centenaries of Sherlock
Holmes and Oscar Wilde occurred within a few months of
each other in 1954. That these two eminent figures of the
later Victorian era should have been saluted in the same
year was less singular than might at first have been supposed; for there were numerous parallels in their careers.
Not the least of these was the basic (or should one say
'elementary'?) fact that the birth year of both has been
disputed. Although the majority view favours 1954 for
Holmes's centenary there are dissentients who have suggested other dates; and despite the consensus of Wilde's
biographers for 1954 and the official celebrations in that
year, some writers and reference books have repeatedly
given 1856 as the year of his birth. Nor would it be too
fanciful to detect fugitive identities elsewhere. Both could
claim artistic descent; Holmes from Vernet, the French
painter; Wilde through his remarkable poet-mother,
'Speranza'. Both had a highly-developed sense of the
dramatic. Both could assume aliases — Holmes as Captain
Basil, Wilde as Sebastian Melmoth. Both in their heyday
were courted by the rich and famous. Both had royal links;
Wilde, as we now know, being the godson of the King of
Sweden; while Holmes was the confidant of the heads of
several reigning houses.

But it is perhaps better to analyse these correspon-
dences in some kind of sequence. One goes back, therefore, to the best-known of the contacts, to the London
dinner at which a representative of the Philadelphia
publishing firm of J. B. Lippencott & Co. invited Wilde
and Conan Doyle each to write a novel for the company's
monthly magazine. From that meeting (surely one of the
oddest encounters in a decade of oddity) emerged *The*

Picture of Dorian Gray and *The Sign of Four*. Both were published in Lippincott's magazine during 1890 and some critics have fancied that they could detect unusual Wildean echoes in the Sherlock Holmes story. Although in a later adventure Holmes brutally orders Watson to 'cut out the poetry', he himself is claimed to have become somewhat lyrical in describing dawn over London in the *Sign*:

'How sweet the morning air is! See how that one little cloud floats like a pink feather from some gigantic flamingo. Now the red rim of the sun pushes itself over the London cloud-bank.'

But this was not really Holmes' line and one must admit that Wilde did the thing much better when, as Lord Arthur Savile saw the Covent Garden wagons in the dawn, 'the great piles of vegetables looked like masses of jade against the morning sky, like masses of green jade against the pink petals of some marvellous rose'. (In passing one may note that the volume of Lippincott which printed *Dorian Gray* contained also *A Marriage at Sea* by J. Clark Russell, a writer whose fine sea stories were, as we know, among Dr Watson's favourite reading. Some enthusiast, whose knowledge of London's by-ways is as extensive as the Master's, should also investigate the possible affinity between the East End opium den frequented by Dorian Gray and 'The Bar of Gold' where Holmes and Watson improbably met in the adventure of *The Man With the Twisted Lip*.)

If there is no evidence that Wilde and Holmes ever actually saw each other, there is at least some probability. Indeed if it be accepted that Holmes went to Oxford rather than Cambridge (and Sir Sidney Roberts, Gavin Brend and Mgr Knox are among the Sherlockian scholars who have claimed this for him), they would have been contemporary and Wilde, who had a connoisseur's instinct for ancient lineage, could not have failed to be impressed by so aristocratic a personage as Reggie Musgrave who reminded even the undemonstrative Holmes of 'grey archways and mullioned windows and all the venerable wreckage of a feudal keep'. Nor would it have been remarkable if when Holmes and Watson encountered the black-bearded passenger in the hansom during their morning stroll down Regent Street they had seen Wilde in a neighbouring cab en route for lunch at the Cafe Royal which was one of his favourite restaurants. (Holmes and Wilde were both prodigious hansom takers.) On the summer evening when Holmes and Watson sauntered along Pall Mall to meet Mycroft at the Diogenes they might also have run into Wilde who belonged to a club in Albemarle Street and had rooms in St James's. Wilde incidentally took his degree at Oxford in the same year that Dr Watson took his at London University. When Wilde first came up to London he occupied rooms 'in a dingy street off the Strand' and so may have been a near neighbour of Watson who was leading a 'comfortless meaningless existence at a private hotel in the Strand'.

Early in 1881 Holmes and Watson entered upon their immortal partnership at 221B and on March 4th set out for Lauriston Gardens, Brixton, on the investigation of the mysterious murder which was to mark the opening of their long series of exploits. It is not clear whether Watson's literary ambitions had emerged at that period. Holmes, however, was already an occasional contributor to the magazines, for it was his article 'The Book of Life' which Watson characterized as 'ineffable twaddle'. Wilde also had by then entered the literary field, for two days before Watson's outburst one of his poems had been published in *The World*, the gossipy periodical in which Wilde and Whistler were later to indulge some not very dignified slanging. (In Mycroft's exhortation to his brother in *The Bruce-Partington Plans*: 'Never mind your usual petty puzzles of the police court', one somehow detects an echo of Whistler's waspish and ill-deserved sneer: 'Oscar picks from our platters the plums for the pudding he peddles in the provinces.')

It was also in this year of 1881 that 'Patience' opened its long run at the Opera Comique and that *Punch* began its frequent, and often exceedingly crude, attacks on Wilde (On September 17, 1881, a parody of a Wilde poem was described as 'stanzas by our muchly admired Poet, Drawit Milde'!) In February of the following year at about the time when Alexander Holder, the banker, was splashing through the snow to consult Holmes about the beryl coronet, Wilde was driving a masterful snowplough through the prejudices of North American audiences on his now famous tour. Dr Watson would of course have noted that during this progression Wilde visited one of his own heroes, the Rev. Henry Ward Beecher, whose unframed portrait stood on top of the books in the sitting room at 221B.

We may be sure that Holmes and Watson, who read all the papers and kept an extensive index of cuttings, took proper account of Wilde's increasing stature as a serious poet and literary and dramatic critic in the immediately succeeding years. One fancies that with their taste for good living they would especially have relished his article 'Dinners and Diners' which appeared in the *Pall Mall*

Gazette on March 7, 1885. And what an intriguing under-lining of our present speculation is opened up by Wilde's anonymous article in the *Court and Society Review* for May 4, 1887: 'Should Geniuses Meet?'

Meanwhile the coincidences continued. On April 13, 1887, Wilde reviewed William Gillette's drama 'Held by the Enemy'. Who could have guessed that before the century was out, Gillette would have written another play with Sherlock Holmes as hero — a best-seller in at least two continents? Readers of *The Sign of Four* will recall that Miss Morstan, later to become the wife of Dr Watson, had a rendezvous under the portico of the Lyceum Theatre in Wellington Street, Strand, as the crowds were arriving in the drizzly dusk of a 'September' day in 1887. It is quite possible that Wilde himself was at the theatre that very evening, for on September 14, 1887, the *Court and Society Review* published his notice of 'The Winter's Tale' at the Lyceum. (In passing it is pertinent to recall that Audrey Beardsley's *Yellow Book* drawing 'Lady Gold's Escort' is set in the portico of this theatre. Another of his well-known drawings, 'The Wagnerites', poses the further inquiry as to whether Holmes and Watson ever met the marvellous boy. We know that Beardsley was an ardent worshipper of Wagner; we know that Holmes and Watson were opera-goers and that at the end of *The Red-headed League* they went to a Wagner night at Covent Garden. It is pretty certain that Holmes, with his special interest in art, must have noted the phenomenal flowering of this young genius of the nineties.)

Also in 1887 Holmes investigated the affairs of Lord Robert St Simon and Wilde wrote an account of the crime of Lord Arthur Savile. These two young London noblemen were doubtless acquainted. In the following year, at about the time that *The Times* was congratulating Wilde on his editing of *Woman's World*, Holmes was telling Watson (*Second Stain*) 'the fair sex is your department'.

Parallelism reached its peak of fame, however, in 1893 when both Holmes and Wilde were twice parodied in the same issues of *Punch*. On August 26 appeared an 'Adventure of Picklock Holes' together with a discussion of Oscar's newest comedy under the not-very subtle title of 'Still Wilder Ideas'. Then, in the New Year's Eve issue, came another Picklock Holes story and yet another burlesque of Wilde in which Dorian Gray was seen taking Juliet in to dinner in the company of Richard Feverel, Ethel Newcome, Ernest Maltravers and Tom Jones.

I shall not elaborate on the coincidences that Robert Ross, Wilde's literary executor, once published an article entitled 'The Landscapes of Mr Holmes'; that Lord Alfred Douglas, like Watson, was a Turf addict and had an account at Cox's; or that Wilde's marriage at St James's, Sussex Gardens, Paddington, was in the same neighbourhood as Irene Adler's at St Monica's, Edgeware Road. But I may be permitted to point to numerous parallels among the characters of these two, otherwise how different, worlds. One could claim, for example, that Lady Windermere had at least a topographical affinity with Langdale Pike, the gossip-writer of *The Illustrious Client*. Lady Windermere's London home was called Bentinck House. It was doubtless in Bentinck Street where Holmes had a narrow escape from the whizzing van. Parker, the Windermere's butler might have been related to the performer on the jew's harp, who kept watch in the 'empty house'. The Hon. Gwendolen Fairfax, is almost a blood-relative of 'Lady Frances Carfax', while Sir Robert Chiltern, Bart, Under-Secretary for Foreign Affairs (*An Ideal Husband*) was obviously a contemporary of the Rt Hon. Trelawney Hope, Secretary for European Affairs. When, in *The Canterville Ghost*, we read, 'He rubbed out the stain a second time', we take the allusion without hesitation, while young Washington Otis's letter on the subject of 'The Permanence of Sanguineous Stains when connected with Crime' was of course precisely the kind of monograph that Holmes himself might have written. Nor do we require any qualities of master-detection in order to see the significance of this quotation from 'The Sphinx':

'Foul snake and speckled adder . . . crawl'. ⁓

But it is to *Lord Arthur Savile's Crime* (published in 1887, the same year as *A Study in Scarlet*) that we must look for the most striking evidence of affinity between the literature of Baker Street and Tite Street. In the opening scene of the story, for example, there is a duchess who uses one of Watson's favourite expressions, 'Good heavens', and a girl with violet eyes like those of Alice Turner in *The Boscombe Valley Mystery*. The chiromantist's reading of a guest's palm sounds like one of Holmes's own assessments in reverse:

'An adventurous nature; four long voyages in the past, and one to come. Been shipwrecked three times. No, only twice, but in danger of a shipwreck your next journey. A strong Conservative, very punctual and with a passion for collecting curiosities. Had a severe illness between the ages of sixteen and eighteen. Was left a fortune when about 30. Great aversion to cats and Radicals.'

How illuminating also to have compared the palmist's 'elaborate treatise on the subject of the human hand' with

Holmes's own monograph on 'the influence of a trade upon the form of the hand'.

When Lord Arthur went on his nocturnal prowl he must have passed Baker Street, for he walked along by the park, crossed Oxford Street and presently found himself at Marylebone Church. At times the story moreover adopts the authentic idiom of the Sherlockian saga: Lord Arthur *rushes* across the room, *flings* himself into a divan. There are also the familiar touches of a hansom and a policeman with bull's eye-lantern. Later, when the young lord, buying poison at a Mayfair chemist's, explains 'that it was for a large Norwegian mastiff . . . which had already bitten the coachman twice in the leg' we immediately hear overtones of Sigerson, Carlo and Victor Trevor's bull terrier. As we see him disappearing into the club library 'with the *Pall Mall*, the *St James's*, the *Globe*, and the *Echo*', do we not at once recall Holmes's instruction about the goose advertisement in *The Blue Carbuncle*? And when we are told that Lord Arthur visited a Russian who had lodgings in Bloomsbury we naturally recall that both Holmes and Conan Doyle had rooms in that quarter when they first came to London.

Best of all in the story, there is a German anarchist, Herr Winckelkopf, who shares Holmes's taste for something a little choice in white wines ('sipping the most delicious Marcobrunner out of a pale yellow hock glass marked with the Imperial monogram') and his contempt for the police ('I have always found that by relying on their stupidity we can do exactly what we like'). They are also twin-souls on the delicate matter of fees. Winckelkopf: 'I do not work for money; I live entirely for my art.' Holmes: 'It is art for art's sake Watson. I suppose when you doctored you found yourself studying cases without thought of a fee?' (*The Red Circle*.)

One suspects that the explosive barometer which Winckelkopf admitted sending to the military governor of Odessa and which blew a member of the staff to atoms might have been the reason why Holmes, in *A Scandal in Bohemia*, was 'summoned to Odessa in the case of the Trepoff murder'. And there can surely be little doubt that it was another of Herr W.'s pretty inventions, 'an umbrella that went off as soon as it was opened', which liquidated Mr James Phillimore who, as recorded in *Thor Bridge*, 'stepped back into his own house to get his umbrella and was never more seen in this world'. (Robert Ross, by the bye, lived in *Phillimore* Gardens, Kensington, and was once apostrophized by Wilde as 'St Robert of Phillimore'.)

In *Memories and Adventures*, Conan Doyle paid a generous tribute to Wilde's artistry. But when Wilde, exhorting him to see one of his plays, gravely said 'Ah, you must go. It is wonderful. It is genius!' Sir Arthur heavily recorded that he thought Wilde was mad. It apparently did not occur to him that this was Wilde's customary light-hearted banter. One feels that Holmes himself would have managed the occasion more adequately. Oscar was an incomparable conversationalist and Sherlock, as we know from *The Sign of Four*, was no mean performer. ('I have never known him so brilliant. He spoke on a quick succession of subjects — on miracle plays, on medieval pottery, on Stradivarius violins, on the Buddhism of Ceylon, and on the warships of the future — handling each as though he had made a special study of it.')

How memorable such an encounter would have been. The two larger-than-life figures, utterly dissimilar save that both had genius, each a foeman worthy of the other's steel, each a superlative master in his chosen craft, each uniquely representing the opposing poles of the age. But Holmes would doubtless have had the last word, with Wilde as with Watson: 'Art in the blood is liable to take the strangest forms.' (*The Greek Interpreter.*)

A Baker Street Portrait Gallery

One of the most attractive of all Sherlockian illustrations is the 'Reverie' which appeared as the frontispiece to *The Red Circle* in the *Strand*. It shows Holmes in profile surrounded by wraith-like reminiscences of earlier adventures conjured up in the smoke from his pipe. Most of us have our own special pipe dreams about 221B and its fascinating frieze of characters.

Perhaps few things more clearly showed Conan Doyle as a born story-teller than his genius for pin-pointing a personality in a single phrase. That is why we always wish to know more about those peripheral 'extras' who figure so briefly, and sometimes so balefully, in the untold stories of Dr Watson. Do you recall the description of Parker — 'a garrotter by trade, and a remarkable performer on the jews' harp' — who watched 221B for Colonel Moran in the adventure of the empty house? One would like to look closer into his remarkable accomplishments. Parker, by the way, was a testimony to Holmes' memory for faces. Although the Master had been out of the country for three years, and although Parker was apparently only a minor member of the Moriarty organization, he was recognized immediately. Possibly, however, the fellow was whiling away the tedium of his vigil by performing on his jews' harp which would of course have made identification much easier.

There are many similar cameos, illumined for a moment as John Clay, 'murderer, thief, smasher and forger', was caught in the beam of Holmes' dark lantern in the vaults of the City and Suburban Bank. What, for example, of Wilson, the canary trainer, or the teetotaller who threw his false teeth at his wife? Can there have been a more toothsome mystery than the fate of the cutter *Alicia*, 'which sailed one spring morning into a small patch of mist from where she never again emerged'? What dark horrors lie behind the casual hint of 'Ricoletti of the Club Foot and his Abominable Wife' or 'the dreadful business of the Abernetty family' which was first brought to Holmes' notice by the depth which the parsley had sunk into the butter on a hot day? These, like that matter of the Giant Rat of Sumatra, are stories 'for which the world is not yet prepared', and, while Adrian Conan Doyle and John Dickson Carr have given us crisp, workman-like accounts of what might have happened, they do not always — how, indeed, could they? — measure up to one's private imaginings. Unheard melodies are always sweeter.

But if one's fancy dallies delectably on the fringes of the saga, how much more do some of the foreground figures bespeak attention. Thomas Hardy once wrote of 'A Group of Crusted Characters'. The same title might fit these random reflections on some of my favourites in the Baker Street Gallery.

DR JOHN H. WATSON

Behind the long lean figure of Holmes there is always the ampler shadow of Dr Watson. Of Dr Watson, faithful chronicler, to whom we are all so vastly indebted despite his shaky chronology. Always available; ready alike to neglect his health, his wife, his practice or his personal safety at the call of duty. 'Come at once — if convenient — if inconvenient come all the same' wired the peremptory Holmes in a famous telegram and we can have no doubt that Watson would have been there. Who does not warm to the old campaigner as with his service revolver in his pocket he strides alongside Holmes with 'the thrill of adventure in his heart'?

Old campaigner? There are those who hint that the good doctor harped overmuch on his Afghanistan experience and his unstable wounds. They say that as he was disabled at the fatal battle of Maiwand soon after he reached India, he saw little active service. They also wonder how he picked up his 'experience of women in three continents' so early in his career. At least he was able to exploit both facets; for his somewhat rambling accounts of Afghanistan were rapturously received by sweet Mary Morstan, while Holmes recognized his special qualifications by remarking: 'With your natural advantages, Watson, every lady is your helper and accomplice.'

Doubtless because he was familiar with the Criterion Bar plus the chance admission at the opening of *The Sign of Four* about the Beaune he had taken with lunch, Watson has been accused of occasional inebriety. J. P. W. Mallalieu, M.P., for example, has suggested that Big Bob Ferguson threw him over the ropes at Richmond, not because he was playing for Blackheath, but because he was a spectator who had wandered on to the field in his cups and was interrupting the game. Ian M. Leslie has stressed as significant the point that Watson only called to see his friend Holmes on the *second* day after Christmas in *The*

Blue Carbuncle and that when asked to examine the battered bowler hat he replied, 'I can see nothing'. The curious may note that at the close of this adventure, Holmes addresses Watson formally as 'Doctor', a somewhat chilly note between old friends at that season. I think that Holmes suddenly remembered that Watson had been neglectful in not visiting him until the day after Boxing Day and that this was his mild rebuke. Notice, too, that despite their close comradeship they never call each other by their front names. Watson indeed carries this professional air of correctness into his writings and frequently describes the Master as *Mr* Sherlock Holmes.

Wynford Vaughan Thomas has surmised that Watson was really referring to two fondly-remembered pubs on that blazing August morning when he yearned for 'The Glades' of the New Forest or 'The Shingle' of Southsea and that the quotation marks and capital initials have only been omitted from the customary text through the delicacy of his publisher! I have always felt that the whole of the famous thought-reading episode which follows could in fact be interpreted in terms of a Watsonian hang-over. The seasoned campaigner, to whom a thermometer of 90 was ordinarily no hardship, could not on this occasion bear the *reflected* light from a brick wall across the street. Unable to concentrate, he had tossed aside the newspaper without noticing the remarkable account of the ears in the box. Next he fell into a brown study. The broken train of thought, which began when his eye rested on the newly-framed picture of General Gordon, doubtless arose from his recollection that the general sometimes carried a bottle of brandy in one hand to balance the Bible in the other. Add to these significant touches the vacant expression, the flashing eye, the clenching of the fists, the puckered brow, the set lip, the shaking head, the hand stealing towards the old wound and there emerges a sinister and unmistakable portrait. Without doubt the symptoms are those which Holmes immediately detected in Mr Henry Baker in *The Blue Carbuncle* and one wonders whether it was vanity or charity that made him forbear to read them off in Watson. It is clear to me at any rate that Watson was suffering from the father and mother of a hang-over. I believe that the miasma was so colossal that even the memory of it always shook him off balance. Hence the subsequent appalling muddle in allocating this thought-reading episode between *The Cardboard Box* and *The Resident Patient*!

On the theory that a man's hobbies may be revealed by his contempt for those who do not share them, I believe that new light is also thrown on Watson's alleged alcoholism by a passage in *The Naval Treaty*. It is pretty obvious that in his heart of hearts Watson despised young Phelps even though they had been at school together. The fact that he used to 'chivy him about the playground with a cricket-stump' was doubtless the first manifestation of this distaste. The Tadpole's subsequent nepotic career, coupled with his complete lack of manliness would further emphasize the rift. How could the sturdy Watson be in sympathy with so nervous a creature, liable to shriek with delight or kiss one's hand; who, on the loss of the plans, made a scene at his office, arrived home a raving maniac, and was unconscious for nine weeks with brain-fever? So, when Holmes said 'I suppose that man Phelps does not drink?' one could fancy a Colonel Chinstrap quality in Watson's voice as he replied 'I should not think so'.

In passing, I have always been puzzled as to why
Holmes should have 'grassed' Joseph Harrison twice
before recovering the 'naval treaty'. To 'grass' is, of
course, an old sporting term meaning to knock down or to
bring down. (The American omnibus edition reads 'I had
to *grasp* him twice' which is a nonsense.) But to knock a
man down twice may seem excessively rough treatment,
even if he is armed with a long-bladed knife. I believe that
one has to go back to the earlier part of the story for the
explanation. When Holmes and Watson first arrive at
Briarbrae, Woking, they are greeted by Harrison who
says 'Percy has been enquiring for you all the morning.
Ah, poor old chap, he clings to any straw'. This remark
belongs to the category of things which might have been
more happily expressed. Holmes was sure to resent it. I
think he remembered and gave the prospective brother-
in-law an extra one for luck when he got him alone!

A shrewd blow at the theory of Watson's alleged tippling
was delivered by Guy Warrack at one of the annual
dinners of the Sherlock Holmes Society when he recalled
the occasion on which Holmes chided Watson for *not* going
into the local public house to pick up the gossip. There is
no doubt that Watson was sometimes 'cruelly used', as even
Holmes once admitted. He could therefore be forgiven the
occasional extra glass of wine at lunch. Faced with the
pungent chemical experiments, the impromptu violin, the
noisome shag tobacco, the litter of old newspapers, etc.,
one feels that he must have shown either great fortitude of
mind or stark insensibility. In *The Musgrave Ritual* he
mildly comments: 'Not that I am in the least conven-
tional. . . . But with me there is a limit, and when I find
a man who keeps his cigars in the coal-scuttle, his tobacco

in the toe end of a Persian slipper, and his unanswered correspondence transfixed by a jack-knife into the very centre of his wooden mantelpiece, then I begin to give myself virtuous airs.' We may also feel that Watson behaves very calmly when Holmes pokes fun at his ignorance. In *The Final Problem* he is derided because he has never heard of Moriarty or Moran; but he could have retorted that Holmes, for all his omnivorous reading and card-indexing, appeared in turn never to have heard of the Secretary for European Affairs or the Duke of Holdernesse — or why had he to look them up in a directory? Similarly, in *Shoscombe Old Place*, he knows very little about the most daredevil amateur steeplechaser nor that his sister breeds the most famous spaniels in England.

Although Watson is of necessity overshadowed by Holmes in the saga, he nevertheless emerges as a remarkable personality in his own right. 'His stories, like Boswell's *Johnson*, are the records of not one but two great men,' says E. M. Wrong in the introduction to *Stories of Crime and Detection* (The World's Classics). 'His brain remains consistently a trifle below the average; his restraint, devotion and character are constantly above it.' While his admiration for the Master was unquestioned, we may suppose that at times it was tinged with unbelief. A. A. Milne pictured Watson calmly acquiescing in Holmes' deduction that he had visited the Turkish baths and not the bootmaker since his boots were nearly new. 'Holmes, you are wonderful,' he replied, though Milne claimed that he had in fact visited the bootmaker, but to buy a pair of slippers. In the same adventure Holmes rightly deduced from mud splashes on the left sleeve that Watson had sat on the left side of a hansom and wrongly that he must therefore have had a companion. According to Milne, Watson, like most men, preferred to lean against the side of a cab rather than sit upright in the middle!

Apart from Sir Sidney Roberts' classic 'life', many aspects of Watson's career have been carefully examined by other writers. Sir Sidney presented sound reasons for a second marriage; the late H. W. Bell advanced the argument with some evidence for a third. Dorothy Sayers brilliantly suggested that John H. Watson's middle name was Hamish, thus reconciling his wife's reference to him as James in *The Man With the Twisted Lip*. In passing, I have always boggled at having to accept in this story the too-improbable coincidence that on the very night Watson visits an East End opium den in search of a patient, Holmes himself should be in the same place on a different quest. Nevertheless there is no greater testimony to Watson's fidelity to his profession and to Holmes than in this adventure. Everyone sympathizes with his groan when the door-bell rings, for he has had a weary day. Yet, like a true doctor, he is soon posting off to the East End on an errand of humanity. (Was Isa Whitney his sole named patient?) Having performed his task, he forgets or conquers his tiredness on encountering Holmes and they drive together to Lee in Kent. (The only instance of Holmes smoking out-of-doors?) There they cannot have turned in before about 1.30 a.m., yet Watson is wakened at 4.30 by Holmes who has smoked an ounce of shag in the interval. Three hours' sleep in a reeking bedroom after a long and heavy day. I think that Watson on this occasion deserved more than the Master's casual remark: 'Oh, a trusty comrade is always of use. And a chronicler still more so.'

Watson's medical skill has been expertly scrutinized by

Dr Maurice Campbell, of Guy's Hospital. Watson, for all his willingness to hand over his practice at short notice when Holmes beckons, emerges as a well-informed and competent medico; but is it too fanciful to detect in Dr Campbell's reference to his frequent administration of brandy a hint that this is the kind of treatment one would expect from a Bart's man?

Some of his understatements have passed into the language. As, for example, when Holmes, pale and worn, returns at 10 p.m., tears a piece from the loaf, devours it voraciously and washes it down with a long draught of water: ' "You are hungry," I remarked.' A cherished Watsonism also occurs in *Shoscombe Old Place*: 'A quarter of an hour later we found ourselves in what I judged, from the lines of polished barrels behind glass covers, to be the gun-room of the old house.'

But in qualities and failings alike, Watson is always human, never coldly super-human. If he is gallantly a ladies' man, he is also a man's. We like to know that he sometimes spent half his pension on racing and that Holmes always had to lock up his cheque book when he went to play billiards with Thurston. Always the man of action, he pockets his old army revolver or selects his heaviest stick at the drop of a deerstalker. The Master may triumph over the impending violence of Steve Dixie or Neil Gibson, the Gold King, by sheer force of will, but it is Watson who prudently reaches for the poker in the hearth.

Thieves and murderers roam the London fog 'as the tiger does the jungle, unseen until he pounces'. Without lurks the unhallowed dwarf, deadly blow-pipe in hand. Keep away from the window if you value your life, Moriarty's myrmidons are everywhere. Hand on heart, is there any companion in life or literature one would rather have at one's side than John H. Watson, M.D., late of the Indian Medical Service?

MRS HUDSON

It was a blessed day for the world when Holmes and Watson first took up their quarters at 221B early in 1881. For Mrs Hudson, their landlady, the tenancy must have been a matter of pluses and minuses. Flattering indeed when a glossy brougham bearing some distinguished crest drew up at the door; but not without anxiety as she admitted the endless procession of detectives; the ragged band of urchin Irregulars; the ring-at-all-hours summonses of the eccentric, the dubious and the distressed. Odours and malodours of strong tobacco and chemicals must have seeped through the house like a London fog. Meals — especially breakfasts — were frightfully erratic, the tidying of the rooms a nightmare. Holmes would sometimes hang around the place for days while she doubtless flicked an impotent duster in the basement. Even when permitted to turn out the sacred sitting-room she would be watched distrustfully: 'Pray do not disturb those papers. Don't forget my cigars are in the coal-scuttle.'

Yet she bore the burden not merely during the long period of his professional career from 1881 to 1903, but probably also into his retirement; for she was quite possibly the Martha we glimpse in his last recorded adventure in 1914. It is true that with increasing affluence Holmes rewarded her on a princely scale. (Someone ought to undertake a monograph on his finances. In *A Study in Scarlet* he appeared to collect small fees from small fry, but many of his later cases must have brought cheques as substantial as that for £12,000 from the Duke of Holdernesse which he stowed so affectionately in the depths of his inside pocket.)

One would wish to feel that Mrs Hudson was not moved mainly by money. She was doubtless secretly proud of her remarkable tenants and one can imagine that her discreet gossip made her to be a figure of consequence in those shadowy regions where landladies foregather. O. Henry would have given her a sinister cast. He would have told more; but I doubt whether he would have revealed more. The latest headlines would be the natural diet of such a company and we may be sure that the glint in Mrs Hudson's eye would mean that she could add a thing or two if she were so minded. Her loyalty to Holmes was of course beyond question. Someone has suggested that there was no nobler proof of this than when she braved the threat of Colonel Moran's airgun and crawled on hands and knees to move the wax bust in the window. So staunch an ally would scarcely relish the newspaper praise regularly credited to Gregson, Lestrade and Co. 'Scotland Yard — 'Tcha!' she would exclaim with an indignant nod of her bonnet and an angry clatter of encumbering jet. Just as Paget has left us no portrait it is equally noteworthy and regrettable that there is no first-hand account of any significant conversation with Holmes at 221B. We are aware of the depth of her devotion from Watson's record in *The Dying Detective*. But we should like to know something of their day-to-day relationships. About food, for instance. Scattered references to woodcock, pate de foie gras, groups of ancient cobwebby bottles and so on indicate Holmes' appreciation of choice fare. Yet he must have had dislikes as well as preferences. For example, the late Lord Justice

Asquith remarked that fish never appeared on the menu. How did Mrs Hudson contrive all this? Was it by trial and error over the years, or was there a daily consultation? Holmes, though conscious of her virtues, probably treated her with customary severity. His remark in *The Naval Treaty*: 'Her cuisine is a little limited, but she has as good an idea of breakfast as a Scotchwoman,' appears to do less than justice to her offering of curried chicken, ham and eggs with the precious document itself flourished as a centrepiece. What, by the bye, was the purport of Holmes' observation? It could imply that he knew a lot about Scottish cookery; but there is no evidence of his having visited Scotland — if we except the nebulous and un-resolved case of the Grice-Patersons on the island of Uffa. Or he may have meant that Mrs Hudson was a 'Scotch-woman'. There is no positive evidence for this; negatively it seems odd that there is never any hint from Dr Watson that she had what he would have called Highland antecedents.

One would like to know something more about her private life at 221B: when and why she first settled there, who were her earlier lodgers, what rents she charged. In *A Scandal of Bohemia* she is casually referred to by Holmes as 'Mrs Turner'. There is also great opportunity for specula-tion about the page boys in her establishment: the first is mentioned in 1883 and the last 20 years later. The page in *A Case of Identity* is alluded to as 'the boy in buttons' and Sidney Paget's drawing shows him at the moment when Miss Mary Sutherland 'loomed behind his small black figure, like a full-sailed merchantman behind a tiny pilot-boat'. In other stories the boy was sometimes merely called 'the page' and sometimes 'Billy'. Billy Hudson, Billy

Turner, or Billy who? We do not know their surnames, nor how many figured in the dynasty. But at least one of them achieved separate fame; for the page boy's part in an early run of William Gillette's play was filled by a youngster called Charlie Chaplin — a Billy without ballyhoo.

MYCROFT HOLMES

I have always found difficulty in accepting Sherlock's elder brother. Like Moriarty, he is introduced far too casually into the saga: during a desultory conversation ranging from 'golf clubs to the causes of the change in the obliquity of the ecliptic'. It is notable that this conversation occurred 'after tea'; for while there is much of breakfast and dinner at 221B, lunch and tea are seldom specified, doubtless because the partners were out and about during the daytime. Watson is understandably astonished to hear this first reference to Holmes' brother after they have shared the Baker Street menage with all its excitements for several years. He responds with alacrity to Holmes' suggestion that they should call on this almost mythical character at his almost mythical club — the Diogenes — where members are only permitted to speak to each other in the Strangers' Room.

There is a curious point of topography about their stroll to the club which is near the Carlton in Pall Mall. Watson records that in five minutes they were in the street 'walking towards Regent Circus' (i.e. Oxford Circus). This direction suggests that their course would have been down Regent Street and Lower Regent Street and then westward along Pall Mall. Yet a few paragraphs later we read that when they reached Pall Mall they 'walked down it from the St James's end' (i.e. in an easterly direction). This contradiction implies that they cut down to St James's Street via Bond Street or Davies Street — Berkeley Square. If so, the reference to Regent Circus was unnecessary.

The appearance of Mycroft is as remarkable as his introduction into the saga. To begin with, Watson tells us that 'his body was absolutely corpulent' which recalls Edward Lear's self-portrait: 'His body is perfectly spherical; he weareth a runcible hat.' Further, he had 'a broad flat hand, like the flipper of a seal'. In *The Bruce-Partington Plans* his tall and portly form is portrayed as follows:

'Heavily built and massive, there was a suggestion of uncouth physical inertia in the figure, but above this unwieldy frame there was perched a head so masterful in its brow, so firm in its lips, so alert in its steel-grey deep-set eyes, and so subtle in its play of expression, that after the first glance one forgot the gross body and remembered only the dominant mind.'

This could pass for a description of Oscar Wilde as seen by contemporary eyes, just as the account of Thaddeus Sholto, in *The Sign of Four* appears to carry a reminiscence of Swinburne. One wonders whether the description of Mycroft is an echo of Conan Doyle's earlier meeting with Wilde when they were both commissioned to write stories for Lippincott.

Mycroft is represented as congenitally lethargic. His two visits to 221B are as unexpected 'as if you met a tram-car coming along a country lane'. But this does not excuse his extreme and dangerous negligence in *The Greek Interpreter*. Neither his brilliant display of deductive fireworks in the window of the Diogenes, nor the touch of the master in

'Here it is, written with a J pen on royal cream paper by a middle-aged man with a weak constitution' can mask the fact that a man's life may be the price of his inactivity. (Compare the similar tragedy of *The Five Orange Pips* when Sherlock failed the unhappy John Openshaw.) One is tempted at this point to glance at the explanation offered by the late Mgr Knox — that Mycroft was in reality a crook in league with Moriarty.

Either way he was certainly a very odd civil servant. Especially as he rose to such eminence that there were times when he *was* the British Government. As the co-ordinator and professional solver of all Government problems, Mycroft was 'the most indispensable man in the country'. Yet his salary was only four hundred and fifty a year. We are told that his speciality was omniscience. 'We will suppose that a Minister needs information on a point which involves the Navy, India, Canada and the bi-metallic question: he could get his separate advices from various departments upon each, but only Mycroft can focus them all, and say off-hand how each factor would affect the others.' Incidentally it would be fun to set a week-end competition for an official problem turning on these four subjects. Nowadays, under the operation of Parkinson's law, Mycroft's singleton assessment would be superseded by a hastily convened triumvirate of three assistant secretaries from Commonwealth Relations, Admiralty and Treasury. They would assemble in one of those lofty twilit rooms overlooking Horse Guards; the facts would be marshalled without enthusiasm as without bias; one of the three would undertake to circulate a note of conclusions; documents would be shovelled back into shiny black bags; somewhere in the Whitehall hinterland a girl would morosely complain to her typewriter that this was the third night in five she had been kept late; and the next day a precise piece of paper would go up the ladder to the Minister.

I suspect that Mycroft's inertia, like that of his brother, was largely a pose. Even in the relatively peaceful eighties and nineties there was plenty going on, especially as no secret plan ever appeared to be safe from foreign agents. And Mycroft *could* quiver into bustling activity. Who can forget his exhortation to Brother Sherlock in *The Bruce-Partington Plans* when, as well as inventing a famous phrase, his enthusiasm broke into rhyme:

> 'See the people concerned!
> Leave no stone unturned!'

But Mycroft's omniscience was strangely incomplete. To quote his own words: 'From the official point of view it's simply awful.' If he was so important a figure in the Bruce-Partington case, why was he not invoked in the theft of the naval treaty or brought in to reassure the Prime Minister and the Secretary for European Affairs — prophetic title? — in that singular matter of *The Second Stain*. (Perhaps the vital documents disappeared so frequently because the security arrangements of the period were somewhat sketchy. In *The Naval Treaty* a stranger enters the Foreign Office unobserved at night by an unlocked side-door opening from a 'lane'!)

Similarly, there is no hint of Mycroft in those delicate matters of the beryl coronet and the illustrious client. Nor, although he could have been no more than sixty-seven, does he appear to have been recalled to help his brother defeat the Kaiser's minions in that majestic climax

entitled *His Last Bow*. In fact the only other glimpse of
Mycroft is when — 'a fellow with a heavy black cloak
tipped at the collar with red' — he waits at the end of the
Lowther Arcade to drive Watson to Victoria Station in his
small brougham. It is a fitting valedictory: the more so
since he was doubtless wearing his runcible hat.

THE YARD

Holmes, the super-detective had a continuing contempt
for Scotland Yard. For one whose methods involved the
use of the pocket lens and the microscope, the heavy flat-
footed approach of the official Force must have been a
constant irritant. The tone is set early in the first story
when he tells Lestrade and Gregson: 'If a herd of buffaloes
had passed along there could not be a greater mess.' In
The Sign of Four he says: 'I am the last and highest court of
appeal. When Gregson or Lestrade or Athelney Jones are
out of their depth — which, by the way, is their usual
state — the matter is laid before me.' An anthology of the
Master's abuse could be compiled.

Fourteen named detectives march solidly across the
pages of the saga and only two — young Stanley Hopkins
and Inspector Baynes — are given a good word. Even then
the attitude is patronizing. Lestrade is far away the most
prominent figure in the gallery; he appears in fourteen
adventures against three by his rival Tobias Gregson. Yet
he is stigmatized by Holmes as 'absolutely devoid of
reason', while he and Gregson rate no higher praise than
that they are 'the pick of a bad lot'. It is curious to note
that Lestrade and Gregson are found in partnership in
only one story — the first. Can it be that the higher com-

mand suspected that the combination was not wholly seaworthy?

The convention of belittling the Yard, though a trifle tedious at times, runs through a wide range of detective writing. It epitomizes the English relish for cocking a snook at authority. In passing, it would be rewarding to look into Dr Watson's opinion of the Yard. It was Watson, not Holmes, who described Lestrade as rat-faced and ferret-like, Forbes as foxy, and Athelney Jones as fat, plethoric and wheezy. Was this simply an echo of his master's voice; or did Watson feel that even he could compete on level terms?

Part of Holmes' quarrel with the Yard was that he did most of the work while they took all the praise. But if, as he sometime observed, he simply played the game for the game's own sake, the fault was his own. He told Forbes in *The Naval Treaty*: 'Out of my last fifty-three cases my name has only appeared in four, and the police have had all the credit in forty-nine.' But in *The Cardboard Box* we see this seeming self-denial in another light when he says to Lestrade: 'I should prefer that you do not mention my name at all in connection with the case, as I choose to be only associated with those crimes which present some difficulty in their solution.'

Yet Holmes in fact got the personal credit in most of the big cases — an emerald pin from Queen Victoria, a letter of thanks and the Order of the Legion d'Honneur from the French President, a jewelled ring from the reigning family of Holland and so on. One feels that he was not always consistent in his pose of the disinterested amateur. He pocketed a cheque for £12,000 from the Duke of Holdernesse with alacrity; and although he refused to shake hands with the King of Bohemia, he later accepted his gift of an old-gold snuff-box. One might also claim that his own conduct sometimes resembled that of the Yard rather than that of a prince of detectives. He suggested that Lord Holdhurst — Foreign Secretary and the coming Prime Minister — had difficulty in making ends meet and might thus have stolen the naval treaty simply because he had noted that his boots had been re-soled. In the episode of *The Cardboard Box* he examines the two ears minutely, and after sitting for a while in deep meditation remarks that they are not a pair. But as we know that one is a woman's, small and finely formed, and the other sun-burned and discoloured, his observation is not strikingly profound. Dr Grimesby Roylott registered a direct hit when he called Holmes 'the Scotland Yard jack-in-office', for it was still rankling as he straightened the poker after the departure of the crazy doctor: 'Fancy his having the insolence to confound me with the official detective force!'

Against this background it is natural to find Scotland Yard not only sturdily defending its reputation but also putting Holmes in his place. Thirty years ago a Commissioner who was evidently under the impression that Holmes was a mere character of fiction pointed out that in literature the balance of advantage always lay with the amateur detective: he had only to find the key, whereas the police had to provide the lock as well. Today there is an adroitly organized depreciation of Holmes at police headquarters. It is hinted that even by 1895 he was becoming a little out-of-date: didn't appreciate the significance of Bertillon's new and revolutionary system of finger-prints and all that.

Christopher Pulling, a retired senior official, and Sir John Nott-Bower, the former Commissioner, have also dug out of the archives a 'file' which enables the Yard to score a neat reprisal against Holmes. This document contains Gregson's official report on the murder at Lauriston Gardens, Brixton (*A Study in Scarlet*). It concludes: 'I draw attention to the somewhat obstructive attitude adopted by the man Holmes in this case. Mr Holmes has been known to us for some years, having brought cases to our notice from time to time. He is a well-known drug addict, but it is believed that his friend Watson is endeavouring to cure him of this habit. Watson is a qualified doctor who does not appear to have any regular practice.' In sending the report forward, the Assistant Commissioner of the day added the following note for the attention of the Commissioner: 'I spoke to you about this gentleman's conduct some months ago. On the whole he is harmless, and has occasionally provided us with useful contacts; but we shall keep our eyes on him.' The Commissioner added his comment: 'We may hear more of Mr Holmes who seems to be the not unusual type of opinionated busybody.'

The same authors also produced a 'Clerihew':

> Sherlock Holmes thought it rather hard
> That when visiting Scotland Yard,
> He was asked to fill in 'occupation'
> On his form of application.

Holmes may very well have appreciated this ('A touch, Watson — an undeniable touch! I feel a foil as quick and supple as my own'), but as a loyal Sherlockian I felt obliged to retort in kind:

> If Sir John
> Persists in carrying on,
> One will feel at liberty to go on to
> Reveal all Holmes knew of Whitehall 1212.

One cannot avoid seeing the Yard's point of view. Here was Holmes blandly announcing that he had made the air of London sweeter for his presence and tackling 'the Napoleon of crime' more or less single-handed to the accompaniment of a stream of gibes which Watson conscientiously wrote down — and published. Why did not Lestrade drag the fountains in Trafalgar Square for the missing body? 'Is there any point to which you would wish to draw my attention?' asks Inspector Gregory in *Silver Blaze* and is immediately immortalized as the butt of the famous remark about the curious incident of the dog in the night-time. At the same time Holmes persuaded them into all manner of irregularities. Conan Doyle himself suggested that half of the civilian characters in *Silver Blaze* would probably have been jailed and the others warned off the course for life. How much more culpable, then, was the action of Holmes in *The Six Napoleons* when he asked Lestrade's permission to keep the photograph found in the dead man's pocket — especially as it proved to be a photograph of the murderer.

But while recognizing Scotland Yard's claims in part, Sherlockians nevertheless feel entitled to ask what happened in cases where Holmes was *not* called in and the police were left to handle matters themselves. Many people would agree that two of the major unsolved mysteries in the London of Holmes' active career were Jack the Ripper in the 1880's and Peter the Painter in 1910–11. The latter affair began with a gang of foreign burglars tunnelling into a jeweller's shop in Houndsditch. The late Mgr Knox remarked that in this case the police failed to profit from Holmes' example; for while the Master's method, as exemplified in *The Red-headed League*, was to sit quietly at the end of the tunnel and nab the thieves as they emerged, theirs was to beat on the door of the shop and shout 'We believe there is a burglary going on here'. As for the Ripper case, although the East End bristled with police, detectives and bloodhounds, the authorities not only failed to find the criminal but actually lost the bloodhounds!

Had Holmes (assisted of course by Watson, armed with his old Service revolver) been confronted by two such elementary problems, can there be the slightest doubt, etc., etc.? As E. W. Hornung, Conan Doyle's brother-in-law observed: 'Though he might be more humble, there's no police like Holmes.'

But one would not wish to leave the great protagonists on a note of enmity or even, fundamentally, of rivalry. If Holmes could boast that in a thousand cases he had never used his influence wrongly, the Yard could claim equal integrity. Both were necessary, the strong as well as the swift, even if it would have been tartly expressed by Holmes as 'the bludgeon as well as the rapier'. Despite routine defensive exercises, the Yard today still remembers with affection Lestrade's grand gesture of reconciliation at the close of *The Six Napoleons*:

'We are not jealous of you at Scotland Yard. No, sir, we are very proud of you, and if you come down tomorrow there's not a man, from the oldest inspector to the youngest constable, who wouldn't be glad to shake you by the hand.'

Holmes, the cold scientific brain, Holmes, 'the most perfect reasoning and observing machine that the world has seen', was visibly moved on this occasion. 'Thank you, thank you!' he murmured: then, with characteristic recovery: 'Put the pearl in the safe, Watson, and get out the papers of the Conk-Singleton forgery case.'

135

Baker Street By-ways

COLONEL MORAN

Moriarty's right-hand man and picker-up of ill-gotten gains at whist enters the scene with the cards stacked against him. Colonel Sebastian Moran was one of a succession of shady military men in the saga. His membership of three clubs was no mitigation; for such institutions as are mentioned are either eccentric, like the Diogenes, or harbourers of card-sharpers, like the Nonpariel and the Tankerville.

The colonel was originally pencilled on Holmes' card index as 'the second most dangerous man in London' but moved up to first place after the death of Moriarty. (Cf. *The Red-headed League.* John Clay, grandson of a royal duke, was 'the fourth smartest man in London'. Who were the other three?) It is an odd touch that Colonel Moran appears in the index as 'unemployed'. It is even odder to find that he could only have been a mere fifty-four at the date of the airgun episode, for Holmes refers to him as 'so old a shikari' and Watson as 'the fierce old man' who 'with his savage eyes and bristling moustache was wonderfully like a tiger himself'. Watson was in fact shocked to find that the colonel, like himself, was not only once of Her Majesty's Indian Army, but that he had served also in the Afghan campaign.

Sidney Paget's drawings make him to be much older than his years, and I admit that until I suddenly realized his exact age I had had a larger measure of sympathy for the poor old big-game hunter (as he seemed), down on his luck and eking out a living cheating at cards. When he is caught with Von Herder's noiseless airgun, Holmes taunts him excessively and Moran gnashes his teeth in picturesque fury. 'You clever, clever fiend! you cunning, cunning fiend!' he mutters.

Holmes also makes great play about the colonel's calibre as a marksman — 'the best heavy game shot our Eastern Empire ever produced'; 'the best shot in India and I expect that there are few better in London', but in truth no particular skill was required to put a bullet through the head of a sitting target in a first-floor window directly across the street. I believe I could have done it myself. Nor did it call for the iron nerve which he had shown in India by crawling down a drain after a wounded man-eating tiger. In fact, when we recall that Moran had successfully shot the Hon. Ronald Adair a few days earlier in far more exacting circumstances — firing into a second-floor window across the busy thoroughfare of Park Lane — he must have regarded the Baker Street job as a minor, though essential, operation. Can we not detect here a touch of Holmes' incurable habit of over-dramatizing the situation? The old shikari *had* to be a wonder-marksman because he had tried to kill *him*, just as Moriarty had to be a *colossus* of crime because he was pitted against Holmes himself. We may suppose that the colonel was not alone in setting his sights high.

I was reminded of Colonel Moran and the tiger by two episodes in Conan Doyle's own experience. Dickson Carr tells how at the age of five Master Arthur's first literary composition 'concerned swords, guns and pistols, with which a Bengal tiger was intrepidly pursued into a cave'. Norman Douglas has also recorded how Conan Doyle was trapped after crawling into a Roman drain he wished to investigate near Douglas' home in Italy. He was jammed in pitch darkness while endeavouring to wriggle out back-

137

wards. Douglas was on the point of sending for ropes and assistance when Conan Doyle 'gave a more than usually vigorous push backwards with his hands, and I a more than usually vigorous pull; it released him, and he crawled into daylight, looking a little the worse for wear. Here would have been a chance, I thought, for some enemy to brick him up according to the recipe in his story *The New Catacomb*, which, by the way, was inspired by Poe's *Cask of Amontillado*.' I don't know whether there is anything of Colonel Moran in either of these incidents: there is certainly a lot of the adventurous Sir Arthur.

The colonel apparently escaped the death penalty, for according to *The Illustrious Client* he was still alive in 1902. I have always been rather pleased about this, since I continued to feel that Moran was older than he appeared to be in Holmes' index. I think the answer may lie in one of Watson's transcribing errors. He could have copied the year of birth as 1840 when it was really 1830. This would have brought the colonel to the more appropriate age of sixty-four at the time of his arrest and need not have put his military service out of court. Holmes on a famous occasion was undisturbed at the thought that he may have 'commuted' a felony. In the same way, and quite illogically, I have found no regret in realizing that the tree which grew only to a certain height was not after all lopped down.

HORACE HARKER

I have met many Horace Harkers in the purlieus of Fleet Street; senior journalists who were sound and industrious if a little given to garrulity. I believe I am something of a

Horace Harker myself. At any rate, I can fully share his cry from the heart when he finds a murder on his own doorstep and is unable to cope with it: 'All my life I have been collecting other people's news, and now that a real piece of news has come my own way I am so confused and bothered that I can't put two words together.' He also recalls the occasion when 'the stand fell at Doncaster'. He was the only journalist present and his paper the only one that had no account of it as he was too shaken to write anything.

While he is composing himself after his shocking experience at his home in Pitt Street, Kensington, we may concern ourselves with one or two curious points about this story of *The Six Napoleons*. Notice first that although the manager of the Stepney firm which employed Beppo, the murderer, had never known his second name, he was able to spot him immediately in the company's pay-list. I should like to have seen the index to that pay-roll. How do you enter the name of a man who has no surname? As Beppo X? Or was the index conducted on the simple Holmesian principle of first names first as in Victor Lynch, the forger, who was indexed under V?

Another point. How, in driving from Kennington to Stepney, would you pass successively through 'fashionable London, hotel London, theatrical London and literary London'? All these quarters are north of the river, whereas the map suggests that the shorter and more obvious way from Kennington would have been to continue on the south side, crossing for Stepney at London Bridge or Tower Bridge. I think the confusion arises because one of our authors had forgotten that they had reached Kennington and described the route as though it were from

Kensington for which the details are exactly right. This might have been excusable in Conan Doyle, but not surely in Watson who had been in practice in Kensington for some years.

I have always felt that Holmes treated the already distressed Harker rather shabbily by suggesting an entirely false scent: a practice which may not be unknown to reporters in various departments of journalism. Holmes thought he had been rather clever: 'The Press, Watson, is a most valuable institution if you only know how to use it.' I hope that Horace Harker wrote to him pretty sharply and reminded him that the Press would very quickly lose its value as an institution if it were incited to bear false witness in this manner. Incidentally someone ought to do a separate monograph on Holmes and the Press with a special analysis of those endless editions at 221B which he so frequently tossed aside only to retrieve later for his library of cuttings.

Late one night I turned off Kensington High Street with a Sherlockian friend to see if we could find Mr Harker's house in Pitt Street on the way home. Midnight struck as we approached that row of 'flat-chested, respectable and most unromantic dwellings'. We remembered that Mr Harker, of the Central Press Syndicate, often wrote until the early hours of the morning. We remembered, too, that Mr Harker knew not the typewriter. And in the stillness of that quiet little backwater we wondered if we might catch any echo of one of the most remarkable sounds in the saga — that of his pen 'travelling shrilly over the foolscap' as he tried to make up for lost time.

A Baker Street Portrait Gallery

IRENE ADLER

Irene Adler was always referred to by Holmes as *the* woman and it has always seemed to me to be unexpectedly ungallant of Watson to describe her as 'of dubious and questionable memory'. I claim that she emerges with much more credit than any of the three men in the story of *A Scandal in Bohemia*. To begin with, it was not at all flattering that in Holmes' index she should have been sandwiched between a Hebrew rabbi and the author of a monograph on deep-sea fishes. Then, twice in a dozen lines, Holmes speaks of her patronizingly as 'this young person'. When we consider that at the period of the story (1888) Irene was 30 years of age and Holmes only four years older, this superior attitude begins to look somewhat absurd, as Miss Winifred Paget has pointed out.

Nor is it the only piece of nonsense in the adventure. The king of Bohemia, with his mask, his flame-lined cloak and his fur-topped boots is clearly a character from musical comedy and deserved all he got. Nor does Holmes, despite his double disguise and the assistance of what one may describe as 'the St John's Wood Amateur Dramatic Society', cut a very noble figure. Dr Watson, indeed, is the only one of the unhappy trio who has the good grace to feel ashamed of his part. And even Watson hardens his heart in the end and throws a smoke bomb through her window. One may fairly claim that the only dubious and questionable aspect of the adventure was the conduct of the three men principally concerned!

Fortuitous support for 221B having been on the west side of Baker Street is provided by Sidney Paget's drawing of Irene, disguised in ulster and bowler hat. It is one of my favourite illustrations. We know that Irene is walking from north to south since she has followed Holmes and Watson from her home in St John's Wood. Paget shows 221B to be on her right, or west side. Q.E.D. 'Goodnight, Mr Sherlock Holmes.'

HENRY BAKER

I have always felt the warmest sympathy for this fallen man of letters who lurches, not without dignity, athwart the Christmassy pages of *The Blue Carbuncle*. Mr Baker spent his days in the British Museum in labours not as yet identified and his evenings on other pursuits only too well identified in the Alpha Inn 'at the corner of one of the small streets running down to Holborn'. The late Chris Morley believed that the 'Museum Tavern' at the junction of Great Russell Street and Museum Street was the inn which best answered this description. During some years' residence in Bloomsbury, when the 'Museum' became my local, I was totally unaware of this identification. Later, however, I inclined to Gavin Brend's inspired guess that the origin of 'The Alpha' was 'The Plough' half way down Museum Street. He reminded us that alpha was the first star in the constellation of the Plough and recalled that A. G. Gardiner, the great Liberal journalist, used it as a pen-name. With Holmes' French forebears in mind, he might also have recalled that the Plough was at one time the haunt of an artistic group including Nina Hamnett and 'Tiger Woman' Betty May.

Christmas Eve in the Alpha, with its seasonable distribution of birds to the goose-club, must have been almost Dickensian. Indeed, as 'Clerihew' Bentley might have described it:

142

A Baker Street Portrait Gallery

When the boys from the B.M.
Step across at 5 p.m.
'Our good host Windigate'
Supplies the syndicate.

Not quite Dickensian, however; for the late Chris. Morley described *The Blue Carbuncle* exactly and magnificently as 'A Christmas Story Without Slush' and reported that an increasing number of the faithful had made a ritual of reading it annually 'in that warm little hollow between Christmas and the New Year'.

You will recall that early on Christmas morning Henry Baker, who by this time was walking with a slight stagger, lost his hat and goose when set on by a gang of roughs at the corner of Goodge Street and Tottenham Court Road. It is clear that Henry was on the way home from the Alpha which he and his cronies used as a club. We may wonder why a shabbily dressed elderly man in a battered bowler hat should have aroused the displeasure of the mob. The poor fellow was more likely to have been victimized two evenings later when he was obliged to wear a 'Scotch bonnet' which, whether it be what we now describe as a Glengarry or Tam-o-Shanter, must have been alike startlingly unbecoming to his years and gravity. We know, however, that H.B. was a scholar — he quoted Horace to Holmes — and I believe that he was probably singing a snatch of a Latin carol which the gang construed as insult. Sung with a certain emphasis, the refrain of the 'Boar's Head Carol', for example, carries an overtone of mockery:

Caput apri defero
Reddens laudes Domino.

143

There are mysteries about Henry Baker. What had re-duced him to poverty within the life-time of his hat? Why had his wife ceased to love him? These matters are not wholly to be explained in terms of the slight tremor of the hands and the touch of colour in nose and cheek. How could he break a shop-window merely by raising his stick to defend himself? What was his work at the Museum? Where was his home? Surely, impoverished as he was, he would not have walked around in cold winter weather without some kind of shirt?

One may suggest that Holmes' reasoning when con-fronted with Mr Baker's bowler hat also betrayed a slight tremor. He deduced from the size of the hat that the owner was intellectual, whereas he might have been merely hydrocephalic. He inferred from tallow stains on the hat that the owner's house was not lighted by gas; the grease spots might in fact have occurred while Henry was putting coins in his gas meter by candlelight on arriving home in the dark.

When Holmes told Peterson to put the advertisement in 'the *Globe, Star, Pall Mall, St James's Gazette, Evening News, Standard, Echo* and any others that occur to you', he was not allowing the commissionaire a very free hand. I find from a directory of 1889 that there were only three other evening papers and all were of specialized interest. They were the *Evening Corn Trade List* (subscription £5 15s per annum), the *Shipping and Mercantile Gazette* (5d against the ½d and 1d price of the first-named seven) and a financial journal known as the *Evening Post and Daily Recorder*. None of the three would be likely to 'occur' to the commis-sionaire; nor were they the kind that a poor man like Henry Baker would be 'likely to keep an eye on'. It is an incidental comment on changes in newspaper fashion that the fractional reading population of the period had so wide a choice against only three evening papers today.

Henry Baker recovered his goose and his hat from 221B the night the advertisements appeared. Immediately after his departure, Holmes and Watson set off for the Alpha Inn as described in a wonderfully evocative passage:

'It was a bitter night, so we drew on our ulsters and wrapped cravats about our throats. Outside, the stars were shining coldly in a cloudless sky, and the breath of the passers-by blew out into smoke like so many pistol shots. Our footfalls rang out crisply and loudly as we swung through the doctors' quarter. . . .'

Not less seasonable is the interior of 221B with the crackling fire and the windows 'thick with the ice crystals'. There is also a characteristic vignette of Breckenridge's stall at Covent Garden: 'Turning round, we saw a little rat-faced fellow standing in the centre of the circle of yellow light thrown by the swinging lamp.' I always supposed that rat-face would prove to be our old friend Lestrade, but, as you will remember, it was in fact that little shrimp James Ryder! Ryder, rather a pathetic little character, displays remarkable piety: 'For God's sake have mercy', 'For Christ's sake', 'I'll swear it on a Bible', 'God help me, God help me', 'Heaven bless you'.

There are other odd expressions in this favourite story. The commissionaire cries 'Great Lord of Mercy' when he hears that the lost jewel carries a reward of £1,000. Breckenridge says 'Tell it to the King of Proosia'. Any link here with the king of Bohemia? Nor is oddity confined to conversation. It seems unusual that the famous jewel is not mounted on a brooch or pendant since it is merely the size

K   145

Baker Street By-ways

of a bean. What satisfaction could the Countess of Morcar have had in keeping it in a box or safe? Could the fanlight of 221B have 'cast a bright semicircle on the pavement'? Why was Watson 'not particularly hungry' on this bitter evening: had he been fortifying himself again? If Holmes and Watson could walk from Wigmore Street to the Alpha in fifteen minutes, why should it later take half an hour for the cab-drive home from Covent Garden? And, as Ian Leslie has pertinently enquired, how came it that geese were on sale in a market exclusively reserved for fruit, flowers and vegetables?

There is also a puzzling point about Holmes' interrogation of the landlord of the Alpha over a glass of beer — the only recorded visit of the partners to a London public house. I have always felt that they left the inn too abruptly. Holmes ought to have asked more questions. For all he knew, the landlord might have been the receiver of the stolen gem; or Horner and Ryder or even Cathie Cusack might have been regular callers. Holmes was a stranger at the Alpha whereas I knew the landlord pretty well at one time. Yet if I had ventured to suggest that his beer was as good as his geese, I think he would have regarded me somewhat narrowly. And if I had wished 'good health and prosperity to your house' on the strength of a single glass, I think that our good host Windigate, 'ruddy-faced and white-aproned', would have been inclined to turn white-faced and ruddy-aproned!

I believe the explanation of Holmes' singular conduct is that when Henry Baker collected his hat and goose from 221B, he made straight for the Alpha to tell his friends of his good fortune. He took a different route from that of Holmes and Watson — the better way to the Alpha from

146

Wigmore Street would have been along Mortimer Street and Goodge Street, not into Oxford Street — but they walked faster and arrived at the inn first. I think that Holmes was casting around for some means of eliciting further information from the landlord without arousing suspicion when another door opened and he caught a glimpse of a massive head with 'a broad intelligent face, sloping down to a pointed beard of grizzled brown' and surmounted by familiar headgear. Hence his precipitate withdrawal.

That is almost our final apocryphal glimpse of Henry Baker, the man of learning 'who had known ill-usage at the hands of fortune'. One nevertheless pictures him in after-years — on some bright day when the Master is at the peak of his powers and all Europe is ringing with his name — still taking his ease at his inn, nodding quietly over his glass, perhaps even solemnly raising the inextinguishable bowler hat in silent salutation to the adventure which once he shared.

DR LYSANDER STARR *et al*

When Holmes sought to pierce the disguise of 'Killer' Evans of Topeka, Kansas, in *The Three Garridebs*, he trapped him by asking if he remembered 'old Dr Lysander Starr who was Mayor in 1890'. The 'Killer' admitted acquaintance with this mythical person by saying 'Good old Dr Starr. His name is still honoured'.

The 'Killer' would have proved a foeman worthier of Holmes' steel if he had played him at his own game and replied: 'Really Mr Holmes, I think you are confusing him with Colonel Lysander Stark, of Eyford, in Berkshire,

a gentleman of exceeding thinness who figures con-
spicuously in an adventure of yours entitled *The Engineer's
Thumb* and who, like me, had some knowledge of counter-
feit.' Warming to his work, he might have gone on to say:
'That episode, if I mistake not, appeared in the *Strand
Magazine* of March 1892, soon after the appointment as
Administrator of Rhodesia of a Dr — ahem! — Leander
Starr — ahem! — Jameson who, as all history knows, was
later to become the leading actor in the raid which is
inseparably associated with his name.'

The Three Garridebs was not published until 1925 and one
wonders at the mental processes by which the name of
this African pioneer, who, like Conan Doyle himself, was
born in Edinburgh, and who took his medical degree at
London University the year before Watson, was kept a-
flicker in the author's memory for over thirty years. Perhaps there was an echo of Conan Doyle's own experience
during the South African war for John Dickson Carr
has written of him at the hospital at Bloemfontein as
'awakened at dawn by the swing-step of "The British
Grenadiers" and knowing this meant that the Guards
were moving up'.

> ... Of Hector and Lysander
> And such great men as these ... ?

This duplicity, sometimes, indeed, multiplicity, of
names is one of the curious facets of the Sherlock Holmes
stories which may provide a field for rewarding research.
Myself, I can only list some notable examples in the hope
that others may endeavour to track them to their source.

First, then, there is the prevalence of Mortimer in the

stories — Dr Mortimer in *The Hound of the Baskervilles,* Mortimer Tregennis in *The Devil's Foot,* Mortimer Maberley in *The Three Gables,* the Smith-Mortimer Succession Case and Mortimer the gardener, both mentioned in *The Golden Pince-nez.* Finally there is Mortimer Street at the rear of Dr Watson's house into which Holmes takes his departure in *The Final Problem.* (There is a somewhat similar crop of Mortons in the stories.)

One might compare this with the late Christopher Morley's note in *The Baker Street Journal* regarding Holmes' fixation on the number 4. 'When the Baker Street Irregulars finally issue the Baker Street Calendar they have long promised, I almost think the 4th of each month should be rubricated. The sign of the four recurred very strangely in Holmes' cases. It was on January 4th that he first crossed Professor Moriarty's path. It was March 4th that Watson "had good reason to remember". It was the 4th day after the New Year that the orange pips arrived. The first date in the KKK journal was a 4th. On May 4th Sir Charles Baskerville died; and I don't need to remind you that the date of the Reichenbach Fall was May 4th. The case of the Bruce-Partington plans began on the 4th day of fog. Sir Charles Damery called on October 4th. Violet Hunger got £4 per month at Col. Spence Munro's. Jabez Wilson got £4 per week for copying the Encyclopaedia.' A more recent issue of the *Journal* has listed 77 examples of the use of 4 in the saga. I have no clue to this except the too obvious suggestion that as the author's birthday was on May 22nd, we have here a classic example of two and two making four.

I believe, however, that the prevalence of Mortimers occurs because when young Dr Conan Doyle walked each morning from Montague Place, Bloomsbury, to his consulting rooms at No. 2 Devonshire Place, Marylebone, in 1891, he would cross Tottenham Court Road and doubtless walk along Goodge Street, passing thence into *Mortimer* Street which forms its westward extension. Notice that all the Mortimer references occur after he had taken rooms in Devonshire Place. There are none in the two early books — *A Study in Scarlet* or *The Sign of Four*.

But what is one to say of the Violets or the Hudsons?

An American writer has referred to Holmes' hobby of 'violet-collecting' and they certainly make a handsome posy. Violet Smith is *The Solitary Cyclist*; Violet Westbury appears in *The Bruce-Partington Plans*; Violet de Merville (who has been claimed as Watson's second wife) in *The Illustrious Client*; and Violet Hunter is the maiden in distress in *The Copper Beeches* (I wonder if anyone else has noticed that in the earliest Newnes editions she appears as Miss *Violent* Hunter?). In the unforgettable story of *The Speckled Band* the girl victim is Julia Stonor, but when Conan Doyle wrote the stage version twenty years later he renamed her *Violet* Stoner! One might also perhaps include Miss Turner of Boscombe Valley who had violet eyes!

Of the Hudson clan, Mrs Hudson the landlady, is of course the most famous and Hudson, the seaman of *The Gloria Scott*, the most infamous. It has indeed been suggested that this ruffian was her first husband and that she afterwards married a Mr Turner. Then we have Morse Hudson, the dealer in *The Six Napoleons* and Hudson Street, Aldershot, in *The Crooked Man*. Could the explanation be that Hudson's soap powders were being widely advertised on the buses and hoardings at that time?

Wilson was another favourite name. Among at least half-a-dozen in the saga, Jabez Wilson is the simple-minded pawnbroker of *The Red-Headed League*; while the story of another Wilson, 'the notorious canary-trainer whose arrest removed a plaguespot from the east end of London', has been revealed by Adrian Conan Doyle in a fine yarn entitled *The Deptford Horror*.

Among the pairs of names some are poles apart. Parker 'our vicar who stayed at a boarding house in Russell Square' is referred to in *The Dancing Men*. How different a character from his namesake the garrotter whom Holmes recognized spying on 221B in *The Empty House*! Jefferson Hope, the avenging figure of *A Study in Scarlet* had nothing except his name in common with the immaculate top-hatted, frock-coated Rt Hon. Trelawney Hope ('endowed with every beauty of body and mind') who appeared as Secretary for European Affairs in *The Second Stain*. Cartwright, one of the bright boys of The Baker Street Irregulars, could scarcely have found an exemplar in Cartwright, the bank robber of *The Resident Patient*. And it is clear that the sixth Duke of Holdernesse, who married the daughter of Sir Charles Appledore, must have been furious when he later read that Appledore Towers, Hampstead, was the home of Charles Augustus Milverton, 'the worst man in London'. (The Duke made his bow in *The Priory School* in the *Strand* of February 1904. I wonder whether he noticed that in the issue of May 1903 there was a photograph of a false horse-shoe giving the impression of a cow's foot and described as a relic of the Civil War dug out of a moat at Tewkesbury? I don't suppose His Grace was too pleased to find that his own similar museum pieces were not unique.)

Appledore reminds me that there is a hint of repetition among the place names. The Pondicherry postmark of the letter that brings the dreaded Five Orange Pips is echoed by Pondicherry Lodge in *The Sign of Four*. Hatherley Farm in Boscombe Valley bears the same name as the engineer who lost his thumb. And I have often wondered why, when Conan Doyle might have ranged the world from China to Peru, he should have followed the *Question of the Netherland-Sumatra Company*, with the *Giant Rat of Sumatra* and then in *The Dying Detective* have had Holmes pick up a disease from — can you guess? — *Sumatra*.

When one considers the superb picturesqueness of many of the names in the stories, the lack of invention in others is the more remarkable. Take, for instance, the glittering suggestion of Baron Aldelbert Gruner, Louis La Rothiere, Isadora Persano, Clotilde Lothman von Saxe-Meningen and Wilhelm Gottsreich Sigismond von Ormstein, Grand Duke of Cassel-Falstein, and hereditary King of Bohemia. With these splendours in mind, one is the more surprised to find that in a story which casually mentions the Smith-Mortimer Succession there should actually be one character called Mortimer and another called Smith. (There are other Smiths for the looking — Mordecai, the boatman, in *The Sign of Four* and the rascally Culverton in *The Dying Detective*.) Similarly, if one introduces a young lady named *West*bury to the reader, she should not have a fiance named *West* as occurs in *The Bruce-Partington Plans*.

Note also the preoccupation with certain variations on a name — Alexander Holder (banker), John Holder (sergeant), Holdernesse (Duke of) and Holdhurst ('the great Conservative politician'); or the assorted box indicated by Merryweather (*Red-Headed League*), Mrs Merrilow of

Brixton (*Veiled Lodger*), Merridew of Abominable Memory (*Empty House*), Merivale of the Yard (*Shoscombe Old Place*) and Merripit House (*Hound of the Baskervilles*). One could also throw in Lord Merrow whose letter was found in the despatch box in *The Second Stain*.

It would be amusing to see how many characters one could list with names ending in 'son' — Watson, Hudson, Peterson, Jefferson, Big Bob Ferguson, Gregson, Stangerson, Wilson, Joseph Harrison, White Mason, Jacobson. . . . Or to compile pairs of similar front-names — Jabez Wilson (*Red-Headed League*), Sir Jabez Gilchrist (*Three Students*), Josiah Amberley (*Retired Colourman*), Josiah Barnes (*Shoscombe Old Place*). (One would have to undertake, however, not to have previously read Dr Jay Finley Christ's *Irregular Guide to Sherlock Holmes of Baker Street* in which every name in the canon is faithfully recorded in a dual index.)

But indeed there is no end to the number of parallels. With Hatty Doran, Stoke Moran, Hall Pycroft, Bro. Mycroft, Old Shoscombe and Boscombe, and Doctor James Watson and all!

THE 'EXPLOITS'

One of the major impacts on the Sherlockian world in recent years was the publication in 1954 of some of the untold stories of Dr Watson by Adrian Conan Doyle and John Dickson Carr under the title of *The Exploits of Sherlock Holmes*. The authors took a number of the cases which are only given a passing reference in the saga — 'Colonel Warburton's madness', 'the famous card scandal of the Nonpariel club', 'the Addleton tragedy', Holmes' 'summons to Odessa in the case of the Trepoff murder', and so on — and clothed them in character. Such an event was bound to arouse fierce discussion, since any addition to what are known in the U.S.A. as 'the Sacred Writings' was likely to be regarded in much the same light as, say, an attempt to add another chapter to the Acts or Isaiah.

I do not share this view. If scholarly hands have successfully turned to rounding off *Edwin Drood*, I see no reason why we should not welcome new Sherlock Holmes stories which so faithfully reflect the manner of the old. But the general, and I think reasonable, view of Sherlockians is that they cannot strictly be admitted to the canon of the sixty stories any more than can those two borderline mysteries, *The Lost Special* and *The Man with the Watches* which Sir Arthur Conan Doyle himself published in the *Strand* many years ago.

Therefore, although I thoroughly enjoyed the *Exploits*, I have hesitated — in a purely Sherlockian sense — to 'mix fact with fiction' and so have not quoted from them in the text of this book. I cannot give a fairer assessment of the 'Exploits' than the critical piece reproduced below which I wrote for the July 1954 issue of the *Sherlock Holmes Journal* which I then jointly edited with my friend Philip Dalton:

' "Tut," says Holmes to Watson in the opening story of the "Exploits" (p. 12), "it is not the first time my name has been borrowed by others." '

If the Master was not particularly upset, why should we be? Indeed, when one recalls the ceaseless spate of parodies and pastiches which have appeared on both sides of the Atlantic during the past 50 years or so, it is rather odd to find some people holding up hands in sacrilegious horror at the thought of this newest contribution to Sher-lockiana. Where, anyway, could one find collaborators better equipped to do the job? John Dickson Carr has had access to all the papers in the Watsonian tin trunk for his life of Sir Arthur Conan Doyle, while Adrian can claim to be one of the very few people who were present at the chronicling of some of the original cases. Yes, you say, but the new stories have been written for profit. Well, did not Conan Doyle emancipate himself from his bleak opthalmic consulting-room by means of the first adventures? Or, to put it another way, did not Dr Watson seek to supplement his meagre wound-pension through his memoirs of his friend? There is also Dr Johnson's well-known dictum.

Of course, no Sherlockian will ever be wholly satisfied with variations, however original, on the cherished theme. But in attempting to assess the *Exploits* one should keep in mind two factors in fairness to the joint authors. In the first place I think that so much affectionate study has been devoted to the original series that we tend to credit them with something more than they ever intrinsically contained. This being so, I can well imagine that if by some minor miracle half-a-dozen of the veritable 1887–1927 vintage turned up from some forgotten hiding place, there would be immediate complaints that they were not as good as the originals!

In the second place, the authors are in a cleft stick be-cause of the perhaps too rigid attitude of some of the faithful. I have heard grumbles, for instance, because one of the stories makes Watson repeat that he has taken Beaune with his lunch. Yet I believe that the same people would have objected to a contravention of the canon if Graves or Chablis, say, had been substituted.

For my part, I think that the authors mostly use perfectly legitimate methods. I feel, for instance, that it is entirely permissible to introduce another thought-reading episode (*The Red Widow*) since the chain of reasoning is different and ingenious. I rejoice to know that Holmes had a *red* dressing-gown (p. 209) as well as the more familiar ones. I readily accept Pelligrini's and Fratti's (pp. 151 and 227) as restaurants of the period to bracket with Marcini's; just as Corata at Covent Garden (p. 188) is clearly of the same immortal, if unidentifiable, metal as Carina. Similarly, the Duke of Carringford is a credible addition to the 221B peerage, as is Footman Boyce to the rogue's gallery.

There is plenty of good atmosphere in the new stories. *The Deptford Horror* has the authentic crescendo of suspense and need not be too nervous of comparison with its great prototype, despite the improbability of a heavy yellow fog in June. (Gavin Brend has already pointed out that Watson ought not to have referred in this adventure to the *Bruce-Partington Plans* since the latter incident did not occur until the following November!) There is also plenty of good Baker Street weather. Watson himself surely never made a better opening than *The Abbas Ruby*.

'On glancing through my notes, I find it recorded that the night of November 10th saw the first heavy blizzard of the winter of 1886. The day had been dark and cold with a bitter searching wind that moaned against the window and, as the early dusk deepened into night, the street lamps glimmering through the gloom of Baker Street disclosed the first flurries of snow and sleet swirling along the empty glistening pavements.'

Not least among the fascinations of the new collection is

the study of how far the stories conform to and how far they depart from the originals. Thus, for example, in the adventure just quoted there is pretty strong evidence that 221B was sited north of the Marylebone Road. In *The Wax Gamblers* we find that Mrs Watson has become more sardonic about the Master's calls on her husband. ('You must go at once and see to the comfort of Mr Sherlock Holmes for a day or two,' she says. 'Anstruther will always do your work for you.') Watson, we find, has just as keen an eye as ever for the fair sex, while Holmes is as observant as ever. ('He took no part in our conversation save for a remark that the station-master was unhappily married and had recently changed the position of his shaving mirror.') Sometimes indeed, the Master is almost too clever. It is debatable whether a dust smear on a finger tip (p. 34) would have survived a train journey from Somerset and even if it had whether it would have been distinctive enough for Holmes to have based his deductions upon it. In any event it is fallacious to suppose that books are only taken from high shelves in the manner described.

Among additions to knowledge we now know that Holmes studied the effect of Oriental plant poisons on the organic blood-stream (p. 227) and that the travelling cap he wore was indubitably a 'deerstalker' (p. 292). The original language has also been carefully reproduced. Watson *throws* himself into a chair; Holmes *springs* to his feet; Lestrade *claps* a pistol to a man's head — all in the best tradition. I nevertheless retain an impression that this Holmes hums and tuts much more than the original.

Readers of the new stories will find that the dating is more precise than in the canon. There is only one adventure indeed (*Foulkes Rath*) in which we have to find the year from internal evidence. Some of the datings are questionable; in two consecutive stories, for instance, Bell's date of 1886 is accepted for the *Hound* though the weight of the chronologies is against it. On page 80 we have an incident allotted to December 1893! Such errors are doubtless deliberate since Watson's shaky memory was one of his prominent characteristics. But there are two lapses which can scarcely be laid at Watson's door and which really should not have occurred at all. The first line of the publisher's foreword speaks of '*The Strand Magazine* in 1887' whereas it was not published until 1891, and on page 289 Watson is actually made to misspell his wife's maiden name as 'Morston'.